LITTLE DID HE KNOW

STORIES FROM
ANOTHER LIFETIME

BY

JEROME STERN

Break the Road Publishing

BreakTheRoad.com

A Break the Road Publishing Original

Cover design by Jerome Stern
Cover and author photograph © Jerome E. Stern

Book Layout © 2017 BookDesignTemplates.com

Little Did He Know/ Jerome Stern. — First edition.
ISBN 978-0-578-64304-5

LIBRARY OF CONGRESS CATALOGING-IN-PUBLICATION DATA
Names: Stern, Jerome E.
Title: Little Did He Know
Registration Number / Date: TXu002189403 / 2020-02-06

Jerome Stern/Break the Road Publishing
contact@breaktheroad.com
www.BreakTheRoad.com

for Nicole

*One of the reasons that there are so few women's roles
is that men have co-opted them.*

— PAULINE KAEL

CONTENTS

PREFACE

Like a lot of people who catch the writing bug early in life, I knew for certain I'd grow up to become a writer long before I had any idea if I could pull it off. The impulse hit me in the fifth grade, when I attempted a story about a group of stowaways on a rocket ship. I say *attempted* because I got as far as the second paragraph (although I'm pretty sure I also drew the cover art). By my mid-teens, I took a more purposeful approach to writing and began to visualize a wild future for myself as both novelist and film director, having caught that bug too.

Neither career panned out.

There's a terrific, under-appreciated heist movie from the early 1970s called *The Hot Rock*, starring Robert Redford. Redford's trying to steal a diamond, but no matter how elaborate his preparation or foolproof his execution, the "rock" alludes him at every turn. Facing one setback after another—each new bid necessitating a scheme more implausible and outlandish than the last—it ultimately dawns on him that he has a choice: have one more go at the diamond or simply walk away.

I'll resist the urge to spoil the ending here. I'm only referencing the movie to suggest that, over a ten-year period, beginning in 1985, my stubborn pursuit of a writing career followed much the same pattern. I was hellbent on stealing my own variation of a diamond, and, like Redford in *The Hot Rock*, whatever schemes I cooked up routinely fell tantalizingly short. In my case, however—given that my life isn't a movie—I'm free to spoil the ending: I never did manage to get my hands on the diamond.

I turned fifty-four recently (I'm writing these words in June of 2020, halfway through an abysmal year that could easily get worse), and if I were ever crazy enough to take another whack at writing fiction, I'd have, at best, two or three decades ahead of me in which to be productive. That's one way of looking at it, I suppose. But even putting aside the conventional wisdom that writing is a young person's game, it would also require me to effectively ignore my own history as a failed author—and that's not something I'm willing to do anymore. What I'm trying to say is that, while I might not be old in the biological sense, I'm *way* too old for my fantasies.

When I finally gave up on trying to get published, around twenty-five years ago, I found myself stuck in a protracted funk during which I was unwilling to let go of what never was. Regrettably, this phase far exceeded the total number of years I'd lasted as a writer. I was well into my forties before I could even begin to acknowledge that, yes, I had in fact squandered the bulk of my early adulthood working toward an outcome that never materialized. More recently, my priorities have shifted further, and the dream of becoming a full-time writer no longer holds sway over me as it once did; on the other hand, I'd be a fool to pronounce myself free of its gravitational pull.

I was fifteen when I completed my first short story. I typed it out on my father's IBM Selectric (no computers yet, or none in my house anyway) before handing it in to my English teacher, who hated it. That story, thank God, is long gone, either thrown out with old schoolwork or at the bottom of a cardboard box that got flooded in my parents' basement and then tossed. But I can still recall the essential contours of the plot.

A teenager rides the subway into Boston to take pictures for his high school photography assignment. Caught in an unexpected rainstorm, he stumbles upon an abandoned, partially demolished church and, entering its sanctuary to escape the downpour, spots a rotting wooden crucifix leaning against a pile of debris. Sensing that a decaying crucifix in a wet, desolate church would make for an almost too-perfect composition, he's about to snap a picture of it, before abruptly changing his mind: blood has started to flow from Jesus's eyes and hands.

Given my actual experiences, this made no sense whatsoever. I'm Jewish, for starters, and the only churches I'd spent any significant time in while growing up were the medieval ones my parents would drag my brother and me to on our recurring trips to France. All the same, I'm now able to recognize thematic elements in that story that would reappear in just about everything I'd go on to write—notably an over-reliance on voyeuristic protagonists. My characters all seemed to share a frustrating passivity, often stuck in unfamiliar surroundings in which their only course of action was to react to something or someone else. That first effort also serves to remind me of another shortcoming in my approach: how intent I was from the very beginning to choose subjects for which I lacked a clear understanding.

It wasn't until I was nineteen, in 1985, when a story of mine began to show promise (it's the one that opens this collection). Traveling by train after my freshman year of college, I set about to conjure a younger version of myself on that very same train, as if he were standing right across from me. The time-bending, out-of-body sensation I experienced as I filled the pages of a heretofore empty Moleskine notebook felt so intoxicating that, going forward, I was hard-pressed to consider anything beyond my own memories and emotions as grist for my fiction (every so often, I can't help but wonder how my career might have unfolded had I been willing to write from a perspective other than my own). The ensuing ten years rushed past in the blink of an eye, and, upon finishing yet another downbeat story I feared no one would publish, I approached my thirtieth birthday broke, lonely, and acutely unhappy. A period of sober reflection was long overdue, but all of a sudden I couldn't come up with a single compelling reason to keep plugging away.

Looking back these many years later, it's hard to believe I kept at it for as long as it did.

*   *   *   *

Once I got it into my head that I wanted to read my old fiction again, I searched through half a dozen unmarked storage bins in my basement for dot matrix printouts, Zip disks (remember those?), CD-R backups, and external hard drives, retrieving most of the work I'd submitted to magazines and literary journals during the late 1980s and early-to-mid 1990s. Emboldened, I continued to dig until I located all four drafts of a novel from 1992 that seemed to get worse with each iteration. What to do, what to do?

No one would publish these stories. I received so many boilerplate rejection letters within a ten-year span that I could practically recite them by heart. The thing about rejection letters is that they've acquired a romantic sheen in the public's imagination. It's a variant on the good-things-come-to-those-who-wait theory of life, a conviction that seems, at least from my perspective, wholly dependent on eventual success. We've been taught to expect that published authors endured periods of hardship and rejection early on in their careers, while ignoring the fact that these very same realities would necessarily be true for *unpublished* authors as well (minus the happy endings).

What's the value of a discarded short story anyway? What's the point of putting it out into the world after so much time has passed? It was deemed unworthy of publication when it was originally written, so what's changed since then? I struggled with these questions for several weeks, as I read more and more of my old work. And another question kept popping up: *why the fuck did I write these goddamned stories in the first place?*

I may never know the answer to that one. The kid I was back then, determined to mine the awkward, heartsick moments of his life for material, is long gone, his half-baked motivations by now hopelessly inscrutable. My twenty-something self was confessional by nature, willing to admit to anything and everything, guilty of sins I hadn't come close to committing. This strange brew of embellishment and radical honesty was a window that only remained open in me for a brief while, and perhaps it's just as well: middle-aged suburban dads, the demographic to which I'm currently a member in good standing, are often best served keeping our problems to ourselves.

Which is precisely what I *didn't* do during that decade-long spell, when I put my fictional alter egos through one crushing humiliation after another. This remained true even during a gap in short story writing between 1989 and 1992, when I'd moved to Los Angeles to try to break into screenwriting (crashed and burned, again), before eventually channeling my disappointment into my first and, it turns out, only novel (set within the seedy margins of the film industry, naturally). But while my three-year hiatus from short stories wasn't a break from fiction—on the contrary, it was the most prolific period of my life—a formal break would arrive soon enough; and, apart from a few shot-in-the-dark screenwriting attempts (and some blogging) in the years since, it would be permanent.

Don't get me wrong—it wasn't all gloom and doom. In 1993, a literary agent in New York agreed to represent me on the strength of my novel, and submitted it to a handful of publishing houses with reputations for taking chances on new authors. For a few months, things were looking up, until, as it was recounted to me at the time, an editor at a major house grew so infuriated with the main character in my novel that he flung the manuscript across his office.

My followup effort was such an obvious misfire that my agent and I parted ways over it (many of her suggestions were subsequently incorporated into the version of "Little Did He Know" that anchors this book —but by then I was on my own). Each nakedly autobiographical version of myself I'd been plugging into stories and scripts seemed incapable of achieving the least bit of meaningful progress in his life, and, by 1995, I was coming around to the notion that my characters might be getting on people's nerves. And in case anyone is wondering: yes, the irony of my situation was entirely lost on me at the time.

With the benefit of hindsight, I'm now able to view this collection for what it may have been all along: a cohesively flowing, undivided narrative, one extended journey through a pivotal period in my life, during which every detail seemed more or less connected. I must've had an inkling all along, at least on a subconscious level, that a decade's worth of stories might one day end up merging so seamlessly. After all, I'd relied heavily on alter egos in my work, characters who, by their very nature, reflected the personality of their author.

What I didn't count on was that, when stitched together in the order in which they were written, these tales would so vividly track my own desperation and loneliness over a ten-year period. I've never been one to keep a journal or diary, and didn't capture nearly as many photos in those days as I'm capable of now with just the cellphone in my pocket. These stories are, quite literally, among the only records I kept from those turbulent days. Perhaps, when I wrote these, I took for granted that I was merely depicting my own romantic stumbles, both real and imagined, to comic effect; decades on, it's apparent, at least to me, that I was aiming for something a bit more consequential than that.

And yet, I'm still unable to settle on a satisfactory reason to publish these stories now. As convenient as it would be to describe this collection as an effort to honor the kid I once was, that sounds like something I'd say to a therapist (or the other way around). A more accurate explanation might just be that I couldn't pump the brakes, no matter how hard I tried. Is that called inertia? I can't remember.

THE DAY I MET HOLDEN CAULFIELD

From the green tinted windows of the train, opposite the bar where businessmen are reading their newspapers and adjusting their ties, I can see the countryside. I'm not going to waste anybody's time describing the countryside—readers tend to skip over the wordy parts at the beginnings of stories anyway—other than to list a few highlights: weathered, angular farmhouses, endless rows of wheat and corn, black soil, swaying fields of tall grass (the kind you want to run through with your favorite girl, leaving paths of flattened blades behind you; and when you get tired, you can stomp up and down in the same spot to create a clearing, lie beside her, and rest your head on her beating chest), and extremely lazy cows.

That's it. That's what I see. The countryside. Except most people already have an image in their minds of what the countryside looks like, so I could've just as easily crossed out half that previous paragraph without depriving anyone of my keen and penetrating insights.

But that's risky too, because then some readers might complain there isn't *enough* description. They'd feel cheated and accuse me of taking shortcuts. "He can't just say *countryside* without describing it," some know-it-all might argue; or: "Who's he trying to fool with this amateurish crap?" For the record, I'm not trying to fool anyone. I'm just nervous about putting a lot of work into describing something, only to have a bunch of lazy clichés to show for my efforts. It's kind of a recurring fear of mine that ambition and desire may not be enough to compensate for lack of skill.

A few feet away in the café car stands a middle-aged businessman, fixated, like me, on passing farmhouses, a copy of some financial journal under his arm. You don't want to know what *he's* thinking too, do you? Because I can do that, you know. I can drop into anyone's head I please and tell you precisely what's on his mind (or make it up, anyway). But then you might accuse me of not sticking to a single point of view. "Suddenly this joker's got the telepathic ability to read another person's *thoughts*?" you might say. "Who does he think he is, *God*?" To be clear, this one's kind of a toss-up; I could go either way. (Okay, I've thought it over for a second or two and decided *not* to enter the mind of the businessman standing next to me.)

In my shirt pocket, I have a pack of *Gauloises*. I guess you could say they belong to me, even though, technically speaking, I didn't buy them. I stole them off the coffee table in my cousin's apartment. I stole his lighter too, although I'll be returning to Paris in a week or so and plan on giving it back to him then, so I don't feel too guilty about taking it.

I may have left out an important piece of information earlier on. I'm in France, okay? I apologize for glossing over that fact—it was an honest mistake. It probably slipped my mind because I was feeling panicky about putting yet another pre-conceived notion into the reader's head. Right away, you'd have pictured some wide-eyed tourist or high school exchange student acting like a fish out of water in a foreign country. Without me even having to *do* anything, you'd have seen the *French* countryside, not just the countryside, with all the requisite associations that go along with that, such as rugged farmers dressed in blue jumpsuits, beat up Citroën *deux chevaux* with goofy eyeball headlights, and lush, rolling hills—all because of that word *French*.

Except it just so happens that I *am* a high school exchange student traveling in France, there *are* a lot of blue dressed farmers dotting the landscape, and most every car *is* a Citroën (with the occasional Renault or Peugeot mixed in). As much as it kills me to admit it, it's no more complicated than that.

Can we get back to the story now? The train, the wheat and corn, the businessman standing next to me, the cigarettes in my shirt pocket—am I painting a clear-enough picture for you? By the way, in case you were wondering, I'm fully aware this might not be the most exciting story in the world. There's far too much exposition, for starters, which get boring real fast if you're not careful. Dialogue is where it's at. So I speak to the businessman standing next to me.

"Where you headed?" I start.

"Strasbourg," he answers.

"Oh yeah? Me too."

"Your first time?" he asks.

"Yeah. I hear it's nice."

"Oh, it's nice all right," he says. "Everything around here is *nice*."

Fine, you caught me: I left out another important detail just then. I'm speaking French to the businessman next to me. I know, I know—you're annoyed with me now because you think I'm trying to be clever. And you'd have a point; I did it on purpose this time. But put yourself in my shoes. If *you* were writing this, would you want to devote *more* paragraphs to a bunch of random particulars at the start of your story, or would you just want to get on with it already? If I'd let it slip at the outset that I was speaking French, you'd have expected answers to a whole assortment of dumb questions, such as: "Hey, is this kid fluent, or can he barely hold up his end of a conversation?" And: "What about his accent—any good?" And once a reader gets sidetracked like that, it's no easy task bringing him back.

Everyone smokes in France, though you probably knew that already. I stole the *Gauloises* from my cousin's apartment because I only recently took up smoking—I figure I'm sixteen and it's now or never—but I'm not yet mentally prepared to walk into a store and buy my own pack. (French kids my age go through about a pack a day, so I'll really need to pick up the pace if I'm going to have any chance of catching up.) The things is, during those few weeks in Paris, hanging out with my cousin and his friends, I *thought* I was smoking, only to discover a short while back that I wasn't inhaling! It turns out the smoke from all those cigarettes never actually made it down to my lungs, was escaping out from between my lips the whole time without me even knowing it.

And when I say a short while back, I mean a *short* while back. I first became aware that I wasn't inhaling about ten minutes before this story began. I was standing exactly where I'm standing now, in the café car of a train heading east to Strasbourg, smoking one of my cousin's cigarettes, staring out the window—feeling cool and French and pretty damn pleased with myself—when all of a sudden the train went through a tunnel. In the temporary darkness, I could see my reflection in the window, and that's when I discovered that the smoke that I *thought* was traveling down to my lungs was seeping out from between my lips instead. God, that depressed me. That's what was on my mind, by the way, at the start of this story when I was staring out the window: I was depressed I couldn't inhale, and too terrified to try again.

A brief note on smoke: back in Paris, I sensed something might be a little off. When the smoke left my mouth, it looked kind of lazy and uncooperative. It had no shape to it, and would drift off in whichever direction the wind happened to take it. But when my cousin and his friends exhaled, *their* smoke would shoot out their mouths like water from a hose, forming these long, cone-shaped clouds that would cut through the air for what seemed like an eternity before finally breaking apart. That should've been a dead giveaway I wasn't doing it right. I never got my smoke to do anything like *that*.

Working up the courage to try again, I ask the businessman next to me, who wasn't around for my previous cigarette, if he wants one too. Cigarettes are nice in that way: you can share them with complete strangers.

"*Bien sûr, je vais en prendre une,*" he says. "*Merci.*"

I light the businessman's cigarette first, and watch as smoke shoots out his mouth like water from a hose, to repeat my own stupid metaphor or simile or analogy, or whatever the hell that's supposed to be.

When it's my turn to light up, I take the deepest drag I can muster, but it's no use. The smoke remains stuck inside my mouth just like during all those other botched attempts. Except this time I'm *aware* of what's happening; I can *feel* the smoke refusing to travel down to my lungs. So I shut my lips tightly, and, with all that smoke still trapped inside my mouth, suck in as hard as I can. My lungs scream out as if they're being ripped apart, and next thing I know I'm coughing out smoke— and I mean, it's *loud*—while grabbing onto the railing under the windows for support. Everyone in the café car turns in my direction, and the businessman next to me laughs his ass off.

I try to mask my embarrassment by laughing along with him, but pretty soon the smoke I coughed up floats straight into my eyes. Maybe it's the embarrassment or maybe it's the smoke in my eyes—or some combination of both—but now I'm crying like a baby, so I lower my head to hide the tears before sprinting through the car to the next section of the train, and the next section after that.

Eventually, I stop running. It's now or never, I tell myself, still petrified, tears still streaming down my face. I've got no choice but to take another drag off the goddamned cigarette. But it's still no good. The only way I'm ever going to make this work is if I turn the whole operation into a three-step process: deep drag, trap the smoke inside my mouth, suck in as hard as I can.

My lungs burn, but I refuse to cough. When I finally exhale, the smoke leaves my mouth the way it's supposed to: like water from a goddamned hose. So I do it again, and again, until reaching the end of what I suppose is my first real cigarette. I'm so dizzy afterwards, I can't decide whether to puke or pass out.

I meet Holden Caulfield at the next station. He boards the train and sits in my compartment, right across from me. Other than him being French and all, he looks exactly the way I imagine Holden would look. He's tall, with a crew cut, navy blue blazer, black shoes, white shirt, gray pants, and a striped tie. Also, he has a lot of luggage.

I try not to stare, but it's hard not to. He's clearly a confused kid running away from somewhere or someone or something, and I know for certain the two of us could become fast friends.

But when I offer him a cigarette, he says he doesn't smoke, and I'm greatly disappointed.

1985

THE RIP COUCH

His fingers are already in the developer, already smelling like rotten eggs, as he grabs a corner of the resin paper and lays it upside down in the stop bath. Impatient for results, he uses the palm of his hand instead of tongs to nudge the 8-by-10 sheet to the bottom of the fixer tray—the last step before a quick plunge in the water bath. Extracting the paper after a few seconds, he balances it on one of his sleeves, water spilling from the print and trailing him like breadcrumbs as he exits the darkroom to inspect his work.

Mitch studies the black-and-white photograph resting across his arm while squinting from an inescapable fluorescent glare just above his head. It's a picture of his mother. The expression on her face suggests she was in good spirits when he took the picture, although, as was often the case with her, it was impossible to know for sure. The two of them were seated together on the edge of her bed as Mitch was showing off the second-hand Nikon he'd just purchased with the earnings from his weekend job at the deli in Four Corners. His mother asked to look through the viewfinder, but first proceeded to bounce the camera in her hands as if she were gauging the weight of a potato. Mitch held his breath for several terrifying seconds, worried she might drop the camera, and as soon as the Nikon was returned to him, he grabbed focus on his mother's eyes and released the shutter without asking for permission first (ordinarily, he needed her permission before he was allowed to take her picture). As he stands in the middle of his classroom now, examining the results of his treachery, Mitch can't believe his good-fortune: a shot of his mother in which she's not posing or pretending to smile.

His photography teacher barks at him for dripping water onto the linoleum floor, forcing Mitch's immediate retreat into the relative safety of the darkroom. He dries his hands on a filthy towel before swapping out the negative in the tray, setting the timer, adjusting the enlarger's focus knob, and waiting. When the buzzer sounds, another satin sheet of Ilford paper makes its accustomed journey from enlarger to developer to stop bath and fixer, its textured white surface gradually overtaken by grain and shadow.

It's the shot Mitch took in his upstairs bathroom at home, which he shares with his older brother Pete. The bathroom shade was pulled all the way down, plunging the room into near total darkness even as the rest of the house was bathed in morning sun. The resulting print is so dark that even Mitch has a hard time making out the silhouetted shapes of the toilet and sink off to one side, even though he knows every inch of that room by heart. What caught his attention at the time was that the shade wasn't long or wide enough to cover the full span of the windowpane, leaving ample space around the edges for light to sneak through. In the photograph, thin bands of sunlight form a kind of pulsating neon rectangle that appears to levitate in an otherwise darkened room.

There are chemicals all over his hands and in his hair, and he's overdue for a shower. Too tired to soap up, he shuts off the water before steam has a chance to collect on the bathroom mirror. He gathers his stinky, chemical-stained clothes and tosses them into the hamper on the way to his room.

"That you, Mitch?" his brother shouts from downstairs. Pete's in the kitchen, watching television. *He must have gotten home when I was in the shower,* Mitch notes, ignoring his brother. He locks his bedroom door and drops naked onto his bed before realizing that the slats on all the window blinds are still wide open, allowing the neighbors to catch a glimpse of his penis should they be so inclined. His impulse to masturbate is offset by the sudden realization that he might be an exhibitionist. He darts around his room closing the blinds before reaching for the *Playboy* magazine hidden underneath his mattress. Ms. January is about to turn twenty, information he finds troubling. In a couple of years, he'll be older than the centerfolds.

Garlic, basil, olive oil, pine nuts, and parmesan cheese spin around the food processor until they've been pulverized, resembling green soup. Dad dips a wooden spoon into the coarse mixture to taste it.

"You can't get that at the *finest* restaurant," Dad remarks, passing the spoon to Mitch.

Pete's still at the table, watching the evening news. A gas explosion killed eight people in Florida. The phone rings.

"It's for you," Pete says, handing the phone to Mitch.

"I didn't see you today," Jenny says.

"I was in the darkroom most of the afternoon."

"You could die in that place—all those chemicals."

Mitch closes his eyes and presses the phone against his forehead. Dad stops cooking. Pete turns down the volume on the TV set. Sensing their unwelcome attention, Mitch pulls the phone as far into the next room as the cord will allow.

Jenny whispers: "You think if we ever fooled around in that god-awful darkroom we'd get caught?"

"I gotta spit," Mitch says, holding his toothbrush.

Pete dunks his razor into the soapy mixture below. "So spit," he says.

Dad enters the bathroom and tells them to hurry. Mitch leans over the sink and spits. Dad, standing behind them, uses the mirror to adjust his tie. Pete cuts himself and winces—a single drop of blood glides across his cheek, trickles down his neck, and lands in the cloudy water below. All three of their faces are contained within the confines of the mirror, Mitch observes, wishing for his camera.

Snow hits their windshield and bounces off. To Mitch, the snowflakes look like stars and their car is traveling through space. At a yellow light, Pete accelerates instead of slowing down. "It's the next left," Dad says, reaching into his coat pocket for a cigarette.

Dad tells Pete and Mitch to wait by the nurse's station for about a minute before coming in. Pete reads a brochure about donating blood, says he could sure use the extra cash. Mitch settles into an armchair across from a mini refrigerator. He knows what's inside the refrigerator—he's opened it before. There's custard, jello, apple sauce, apple juice, and grape juice inside. There might be rice pudding, but probably not; a nurse told him during a recent visit that rice pudding is always the first thing to run out.

"*Boys*," she says, smiling, "It's so great to see you."

"You look good, Mom."

"Yeah, you look good."

"God, so many flowers," Pete says.

"Yeah, Mom. You're being surrounded."

They approach her elevated bed one at a time to give their mother a kiss.

Mitch takes the keys, the cigarettes, and the car. There's snow on the lawns but not on the roads. An unlit Camel hangs from his lips, bobbing up and down in time with the song on the radio. He parks a block from Jenny's house and shuts off the engine; for a split second, thinks he can hear snowflakes as they hit the ground.

Mr. Zimmerman sips his whiskey, ice trembling in his glass.

"Jenny, your friend is here."

"Coming!"

"How's everything, Mitch?" Mr. Zimmerman asks.

"Can't complain."

"Still taking pictures?"

"Yes sir."

"I used to do a little of that myself. Even had my own darkroom."

"Really?"

"I was your age. What are you, eighteen?"

"Seventeen."

"Well, I was eighteen. My father and I hammered away at 2-by-4's for about a week, building the damn thing so it would be lightproof. But then I went off to college. I'm pretty sure I used it once. Yes, that's right, I used it once."

Jenny instructs him to close his eyes before grabbing onto his shirt and pulling him towards the refrigerator; Mitch can feel her lips on his eyelids.

"Was that lemonade you wanted?" she asks him, her voice artificially raised to give the impression they're standing many feet apart.

"Yeah, lemonade," he says just as loudly, before kissing her on the mouth.

He blows softly into her ear as she looks up at the ceiling, suppressing a grin. In the next instant, he can feel her hand on his jeans, touching his erection. The back of her head is brushing up against assorted magnets on the refrigerator door.

"I'm heading upstairs," Mr. Zimmerman announces from down the hall, "so Mitch will have to leave now."

"Just let him finish his lemonade, Daddy," Jenny pleads.

"Hey, it's me," Mitch says. "Is it too late to call?"

Perry yawns. "You woke up my mom. She's pissed."

"I had her up against the fridge."

"You didn't."

"I did."

"Then what?"

"She touched it."

"No!"

"Yes."

"Over the pants or under?"

"Over."

"Well, that's good. That's a start."

"Her dad was in the next room."

"Jesus, Mitch. Holy shit!"

"I thought he'd hear us for sure. The magnets kept falling off the fridge."

He stomps his feet on the ceramic tiles in the foyer to dislodge snow from his boots and jeans. Dad rushes over to help him remove his boots.

"Your face is all red," Dad says.

"I did the driveway," Mitch says.

"You did the driveway," Dad repeats, conveying appreciation and perhaps a bit of surprise.

Dad reaches for his coat. Mitch sits at the bottom of the staircase, still catching his breath. Pete leans against a wall, his hands in his pockets.

"I'm off," Dad says. "I'll call from the hospital."

A quartz heater warms Mitch's feet. Pete enters the kitchen, wearing his hat and gloves.

"If you need to reach me," Pete says, "ask for P.J."

"Who's P.J.?"

"Me, stupid."

The phone rings.

"I'm already gone," Pete tells him.

"Isn't it great?" Jenny asks.

"What?"

"The *snow day*, dummy."

"Oh, right."

"You want to come over? My parents will be away the entire day!"

"Mine too," Mitch responds.

A handwritten note taped to a brick wall reads: "Green Line out of service." Mitch follows a street that runs parallel to the tracks for several miles. There isn't a car in sight. He passes toppled trees in the woods beyond the tracks that must've split in half during the storm, heavy snow pressing down on them until they snapped.

"You're freezing," Jenny says.

"Yeah."

"You're shivering."

"It's a long walk."

"Your nose is running."

"It is?"

"See for yourself."

"I guess it is. Do you have a tissue?"

"You know what you should do?"

"What?"

"Take a shower."

"What for?"

"To warm up, silly. A few minutes under that hot water and you'll be as good as new."

His toes are pink.

"Wait a sec," Jenny says from outside the bathroom door. "Hand me all your things and I'll toss them in the dryer."

He hesitates before gathering up his wet clothes and opening the door. Jenny's arm extends into the bathroom, nearly touching his naked leg.

Snowdrifts have accumulated high enough to envelop the basement in semidarkness, but Jenny doesn't switch on a light. She removes his clothes from the dryer at the bottom of the stairs as Mitch looks on, wrapped in a towel. Jenny volunteers to turn away as he gets dressed.

"This used to be everyone's favorite room in the house," she sighs, pointing to the pingpong table in the center of the basement, "until my parents decided to turn *that* into a storage unit."

Bankers boxes too numerous to count are stacked high atop the pingpong table, nearly to the ceiling.

"I miss coming down here," she adds. "You like the couch?"

In the farthest corner of the basement, Mitch spots what appears to be a green corduroy sofa with dozens of holes in its fabric.

"That thing? It looks a hundred years old."

"We picked it up at a yard sale," she says. "It's my couch."

Some of the holes are so prominent that, even from across the room, Mitch can make out clumps of upholstery poking through.

"It's in awful shape," he says.

"Not when I got it."

"Look at all those holes and rips."

"They're mine," she says.

"You ripped the couch?"

"Not just me."

"Wait, are you saying you *did* rip the couch? Why would you do that?"

Jenny doesn't answer, and draws him nearer to the couch instead.

"Hang on, Jenny. You need to explain yourself."

But she won't.

"Other boys?" he asks. "Did other boys rip the couch?"

Jenny grabs hold of his arms and proceeds to fall backwards onto the couch, bringing him along for the ride. She kisses him in spurts, taking a series of quick breaths in between, as her legs collapse tightly around him. He unbuttons her shirt and discovers, to his astonishment, that she isn't wearing a bra. His fingertips skate across breasts he's never seen before, to her belly button, her shoulders, her back, and eventually to the couch beneath her, toward a patch of fabric without any holes around it. Clawing his fingernails into the upholstery, he digs and digs until it finally gives way.

His feet are once again frozen as he trudges through fresh snowfall on the same strangely desolate road that took him to Jenny's house, but in the opposite direction now. A rare passing car spits wet clumps of heavy snow onto his jeans and boots.

"What are *you* doing here?" Pete asks, standing beside a gas pump.

"I went for a walk."

"What if Dad tried to call?"

"He'll call back."

"Jesus. Look at your ears."

Pete leads Mitch through the garage, to the mechanic's office.

"I'd better get you some hot chocolate," Pete says.

Mitch blows into his hands before kicking off his snow-covered boots.

"You went to Jenny's, didn't you?"

"Yup."

"You little shit—here, drink this."

Mitch takes a sip of hot chocolate; it burns his tongue.

"Mom's in fucking surgery and you went to Jenny's?"

"You went to work."

"It's my *job*, Christ."

A car pulls into the station, and Pete rushes outside to greet his only customer. Mitch turns his attention to a calendar of naked women on the nearest wall, flips ahead to the summer months.

"Hey, lover boy," Pete says.

Mitch spins around; the calendar falls back to February.

"If Dad asks, tell him you went for a walk."

Mitch curls up underneath the soft down comforter on his parents' bed. Next thing he knows, it's dark outside, and the phone is ringing.

"Did I wake you?" Dad asks him.

"Yeah, sorry."

"No, don't apologize. I should have called earlier."

"Is she okay?"

"She's still sleeping. The surgery lasted longer than expected, nearly six hours."

"*Six* hours?"

"Can you believe it? The doctor made a joke, said he's delivered babies in less time."

"Did they take a break in the middle?"

"No, they never do that. They just keep working until they've gotten it all out."

"You were in the waiting room the whole time?"

"Only for the beginning. After an hour or so they sent me upstairs to wait in her room. Even *they* didn't know how long it would take. They removed both breasts."

"*Both?*"

"They had to. No choice. Is Pete still at work?"

"Until six."

"Call him. Tell him everything's okay."

"They just left you alone like that, without any explanation?"

"They sure did, and, believe me, I was going out of my goddamned mind. A nurse stopped by at one point to let me know the surgery was taking longer than expected, and I started to scream at her."

"You screamed at a nurse?"

"Not my proudest moment, that's for sure."

"What'd you say to her?"

"I must've been hysterical. I asked her all sorts of questions she couldn't possibly have known the answers to. She just stood there, letting me get it out of my system, before very politely informing me that if I didn't lower my voice in the next few seconds she'd have no choice but to punch me in the face."

"Anyone can take a good picture," Mitch's photography teacher likes to say. "Prove to me you can take a *hundred* good pictures." Mitch's camera is mounted on a tripod. Dad leans against the car and lights another cigarette. The street, sidewalks, branches, and streetlights are all blanketed by moonlit snow, and it's still coming down hard. Each snowflake is the size of a dime.

"Are you sure it's okay to get your camera wet?" Dad asks.

"I'm sure. These things are built like tanks. Wow, look at that tree!"

An old birch in the background of the shot he's composing is about to topple over. One more coating of oversized snowflakes and it's a goner.

"Seriously," Dad says, "I'm worried about your new camera."

"I just need to keep the shutter open a few seconds longer," Mitch says, "so the snow will look like streaks."

33

1986

THESE THINGS HAPPEN

Maybe we're real and maybe we're not—I'm not convinced either way. I want my life to be real, but sometimes I can't shake the feeling that I'm making the whole thing up. What if I'm actually asleep, *right now*, and my thoughts and recollections are some kind of ultra-realistic projection of my dreams? I know that sounds crazy, but I worry about it anyway. I have loads of dreams—my parents say too many. I have all the different kinds: the sleeping kind, the waking kind, the recurring kind. And that's not even taking into account those moments from my life I assumed were real as they were happening, only to suspect afterwards they were instead the broken-off pieces of another elaborate dream.

Here's how that works: if I experience something unusual or a bit out of the ordinary, my memory of it will get flagged, registering it as distinct somehow from other, more routine memories. Pretty soon, everything about it will start to seem a little different somehow, a little off, causing the entire sequence of events to get rerouted in my brain—and, once that happens, watch out. Because now I've got no way of knowing whether those moments actually took place in real life or were just figments of my imagination. I can't *trust* those memories anymore, even if I started out certain of their veracity.

Example: last year, I fell in love at first sight. That's as truthful a statement as I'm ever likely to make. We sat together on a concrete bench, in the rain—it wasn't a downpour or anything, just a light drizzle—and the raindrops dotted her face like tiny beads of sweat. I can practically one hundred percent guarantee this incident took place exactly as I'm describing it, and yet, one year removed, the scene has taken on a dreamlike quality straight out of a movie. As a matter of fact, it took on the characteristics of a dream *as it was happening*—so how can I possibly know for sure whether any of it was real?

Danny Kaye died today. I saw it on the evening news. They played clips from his most iconic movies, like *The Secret Life of Walter Mitty* and *The Inspector General,* and talked about how, in the latter part of his life, he worked tirelessly in support of children's charities.

As a kid, I used to pass countless Saturday afternoons watching television in my basement, and every so often would stumble upon one of Danny Kaye's classic comedies. My favorite was *The Court Jester;* he was pretty terrific in that one. There were nifty sword fights, not to mention dozens of girls in tight-waisted corsets that pushed their boobs together—always a plus. And I can never get enough of that tongue-twisty, fast paced dialogue that was a staple of Hollywood movies back then.

I was born in 1966 (just missing the baby-boom cutoff), and it's hardly an exaggeration on my part to assert that most people my age don't have much appreciation for Danny Kaye. While he may have appeared on TV shows and commercials throughout my childhood, his biggest movies were released decades earlier, during the forties and fifties—a million years ago as far as my generation is concerned. It's no easy task getting teenagers nowadays to celebrate a quirky comedian from a bygone era, that's for sure, not when everyone's lining up to watch Bill Murray or Eddie Murphy movies instead.

I was only exposed to Danny Kaye to begin with because my parents thought he was whimsical and charming—a *real mensch*—but when was the last time a kid turned to his parents for comedic guidance? All the same, I guess you could say I was a fan of his. I'd seen a bunch of his movies, and had even watched him conduct a symphony orchestra on public television once. And three summers ago, when I was eighteen and he was seventy-one, I met him.

For as long as I can remember, I was dying to visit Los Angeles, especially when I was in high school. Like clockwork at the end of each agonizing school year, I'd beg my mother and father to take us on a trip to the west coast, but my parents, European immigrants and college professors who were drawn to the prestigious universities around Boston like moths to a flame, weren't remotely interested in spending their precious summer breaks in Los Angeles. Hollywood and all it represented to them was beneath their mutual contempt.

So it might seem as if the opportunity to visit L.A. in 1984 fell right out of the sky for me, whereas nothing could be further from the truth. A decade prior, my parents had been close friends with a married couple from our synagogue, staying in touch with them even after they'd relocated to an upscale community in the San Fernando Valley called Woodland Hills, about forty-five minutes outside Los Angeles. The husband was a successful oncologist who could've practiced in any number of renowned Boston hospitals of his choosing; but L.A. called out to him, as it does to certain people, and off they went.

I hardly knew this couple at all, only that *they lived in Los Angeles*, and so, year after year, I'd plead with my parents to secure me an invitation to fly out there for a visit. Naturally, my parents *hated* this idea and wouldn't even stoop to making an inquiry on my behalf. Ultimately, however, I must've worn them down, because, near the end of my senior year in high school, my appeal was finally communicated. And not only was this mysterious L.A. couple eager to host me, they insisted I stay on as their houseguest for an astounding six weeks.

The doctor and his wife had a son and daughter relatively close to me in age, but when I arrived in early July, both kids were already away at overnight camp and not scheduled to return until the end of the month. And that's how it came to pass that my only human interactions for three memorable weeks in California during the summer of 1984 were with a middle-aged couple I barely knew, and Danny Kaye.

I was intimidated from the outset by the giant Woodland Hills mansion where I was staying, not to mention utterly consumed by what I saw as my duty to make a good impression on my hosts. Each day, I would try so hard to behave like the mature, polite, responsible, soon-to-be college freshman my parents had made me out to be that, by the end of the first week, I almost couldn't recognize myself anymore. That's about the moment when I was informed that the one-and-only Danny Kaye was going to be our last minute dinner guest. It was a Friday night, the *shabbat*. The dad, it turns out, was one of Danny Kaye's physicians, and, while I might not have all my facts straight, I'm fairly certain he also treated Danny's wife a few years when *she* got sick. Anyway, the point is, they'd all become friends somehow—though Danny's wife was away for most of that summer (in New York, if memory serves).

I suppose now would be as good a time as any to make a confession: prior to my visit, Los Angeles held a kind of magical status for me. It was the nerve center of movies, and I was already determined to spend the rest of my life there. So I can't stress how necessary it was to my psyche to cross paths with a Famous Person during my stay. No visit to Hollywood would've felt complete without having caught a glimpse of an actual movie star, someone so famous that the mere mention of their name would dazzle all my friends back home.

The mom prepared barbecued swordfish that night, I remember, as I scurried back and forth in her grand kitchen, desperate to appear busy in those crucial moments immediately after the Famous Person stepped through the front door. When Danny Kaye did finally arrive, he was limping noticeably, walking with a cane for support. He had a monstrous boot on his left foot that he wore for reasons I wasn't privy to and didn't dare inquire about. He was slightly taller than me, with tanned, wrinkled skin, a prominent nose, gentle eyes, and long, messy, gray hair. His clothes were made of a dark, heavy, solid-colored material that I assumed must've been all the rage two or three decades prior.

My plan of action for the evening was to speak to Danny as little as possible. While it was true that I wanted, more than anything in the world, to meet a Famous Person, I wasn't about to let myself come across as one of those annoying starstruck types. And so, seated beside him at the backyard patio table for dinner, I made no attempt whatsoever to engage him in conversation, treating him instead as if he were a stranger next to me on a bus.

When Danny Kaye spoke that night, it wasn't to the dad, or to the mom—and it definitely wasn't to *me*—but to all of us, collectively. I'd never seen anyone do that before. I hung on his every word, laughing at each one of his dozens and dozens of jokes. The dad and mom laughed as well, somewhat at my expense, when out of nowhere Danny adopted the whining, stuttering voice of a character he'd once played ages ago who also went by the name Jerome. It didn't bother me though. If anything, I was flattered that he'd even registered my name.

After dinner, we relocated to the living room, where I felt brave enough to ditch my feigned indifference and attempt a direct, face-to-face conversation with Danny Kaye. I have no memory of what I said to him, only that the dad and mom had their eyes on me the entire time, which made me feel unbelievably self-conscious. At one point, I found the nerve (or *chutzpah*, you might say) to tell a joke. I can't remember the exact joke anymore—the whole evening was kind of a blur—but, when I was finished with it, everyone laughed. Everyone, that is, except Danny Kaye. He didn't laugh at all. He just glared at me for what seemed like forever, before remarking, "So, you think you're funny?"

It sounded more to me like an accusation than a question, and I had no idea how to respond. What's the right answer to a question like that anyway? Instinctively, I began to laugh, hoping to diffuse the tension, but this only seemed to have the opposite effect. "Ask me this," he demanded to know, his voice booming, "ask me why the Polish don't make good comedians." So I did; I asked him, "Why don't the Polish —"

"Timing!" he blurted out, and we all roared.

Days later, Danny invited the three of us to be his personal guests at a baseball game. The Dodgers were playing the Montreal Expos, and Danny insisted on driving us to the ballpark in his Mercedes, heavy boot and all. We met up in the late afternoon at his tastefully decorated Beverly Hills home, where a smiling housekeeper directed us to wait for Danny in his living room. I stared in amazement at row after row of framed photographs of Danny Kaye standing next to one impossibly Famous Person after another—politicians, movie stars, athletes. It was dizzying. In the pictures, Danny was more often than not dressed in a tuxedo, his hair trimmed short and combed back. The old man who shuffled into the room moments later, leaning against his cane for support, shared the same childlike, delighted expression as his much younger self in all those black-and-white stills, though the heavy boot made it appear as if he were moving in slow motion, and his long, straggly hair, tucked hastily behind his ears, was in serious need of a trim.

The baseball game wasn't set to begin until seven o'clock, but we arrived at the park shortly after five. Using a private entrance that led us improbably to an elevator, we followed a winding corridor on the top floor of the stadium to the office of the team owner, who was expecting us and greeted us warmly. Offering me a ginger ale, he asked me if I'd be so kind as to press the large button on his desk. When the owner of a baseball team asks you to press the button on his desk, you do it, and, next thing I knew, the wall behind him began to hum and shake. Pretty soon, it was splitting in half, separating like a pocket door to reveal a breathtaking view of the entire baseball field. That was wild. Afterwards, we took a tour of the clubhouse and the locker room, where the manager of the team, Tommy Lasorda, shook my hand firmly and presented me with an autographed picture of himself and a baseball signed by the entire team. I was a diehard Red Sox fan, but even I got chills meeting Tommy Lasorda, who at one point took me aside to confide in me how much he admired Danny Kaye, as if I were one of Danny's grandkids or something. I'm pretty sure I was beaming.

From the clubhouse, we entered the dugout and stepped directly out onto the infield to watch the hitters take batting practice. Many of the players already knew Danny and were excited as hell to see him, taking time from their warmups to run up and greet him. It turned out Danny was on a first-name basis with just about every member of the team. I'll never forgot this one guy who bounded up to report that his wife had just given birth to a baby girl. Danny and the player hugged, and then the player promised to raise his daughter on a steady diet of Danny's old movies.

Danny introduced me to the players as a "fine young man," which I got a kick out of—although just then I wished I could've been about ten years younger. That way, the ridiculous fantasy kids have of playing major league baseball when they grow up might've felt a little less ridiculous. But pretty soon I couldn't help myself, and began to picture an idyllic future for myself as a professional ballplayer, trading corny jokes with my teammates, getting limber on the freshly cut outfield grass, and taking batting practice in my pristine blue and white Los Angeles Dodgers uniform.

We couldn't stay out on the field for very long—there was a game to play, after all—and eventually made our way to the owner's private box overlooking the ballpark (I can't remember the guy's name!). Below us, the regular ticket holders who'd begun to trickle into the park had to settle for beer and hotdogs, while we were offered shrimp cocktail, all kinds of drinks, and an assortment of tasty hors d'oeuvres.

Danny had a grin on his face the entire game. Inning after inning, as he breathed in the cool evening air, he kept an intense focus during each at-bat (for my part, I can't even remember who won the game). Before the bottom of the third inning, after he'd shuffled off to the restroom, the owner took the opportunity to share with us how much Danny loved baseball. The owner's wife, who'd recently joined our group, put her hand on my shoulder and added: "He really does love it. It means so much to him. He used to own a team, you know."

"No kidding," I replied. "I had no idea."

"Oh my, yes. Sadly, they kept losing, and Danny was forced to sell."

The owner leaned forward just then, and I sensed that he might want to change the subject. Sure enough, all of a sudden he was dying to know what I planned to study at college.

"I'm majoring in English," I announced, proudly.

"Is that right?" he said. "Did you hear that, honey?"

"Good for you," his wife stated flatly, patting me on my shoulder. Neither of their reactions contained the slightest trace of enthusiasm; I'm pretty sure my response was a huge disappointment to the both of them.

My next chance to see Danny Kaye came about when the dad had to personally deliver some medical results and I asked if I could tag along for the ride. When we arrived at Danny's house, he was in the middle of serving dinner to ten or so friends in his dining room. Danny's housekeeper hurriedly waved us through the foyer, where the scent of sugar, eggs, and lemon was unmistakable, before ushering us into the dining room. Our timing, as they say, was impeccable: Danny burst forth from the kitchen carrying a tall and gorgeous lemon soufflé.

I kept my distance in a far corner of the room, watching as Danny served soufflé to his guests, when, without warning, he spun around in my direction and started shouting, "What are you *doing*?"

"What do you mean?" I mumbled.

His voice grew louder still: "You only have seconds—sit *down!*"

"Where?"

"Quickly, before it falls flat!"

I had no idea what to do next until Danny gestured to the only remaining empty chair in the dining room—his. So I crossed the room with all eyes upon me to sit in Danny's chair, at which point he gently deposited a slice of lemon soufflé onto the plate in front of me. His plate. I ate Danny Kaye's portion of lemon soufflé at his seat at the table, while he stood right behind me facing his guests, who were all laughing at my expense. I was reminded of that first night we'd met, when Danny made a few jokes about my name, but once again I didn't mind, laughing along with everyone else as I devoured that perfect slice.

Afterwards, a woman with dyed blond hair—I found out later she was married to an unbelievably famous record producer whose name I won't repeat—asked me for my initial impressions of Los Angeles. "Oh, I think it's pretty terrific," I admitted to her, as if I were divulging a terrible secret.

"So glad to hear it," she said. "I've never lived anywhere else, but I can promise you this is the most perfect city on earth."

I considered mentioning a few other places she might want to visit, immediately thought better of it, and instead turned away to have a look at Danny, who was gripping his cane firmly, deep in conversation with another guest.

I didn't see him again until almost a month later, sometime toward the end of my stay. After the son and daughter returned home from their overnight camp, I was thrilled to be with kids my own age again. We spent the next three hot summer weeks together, hanging out at their pool, lounging in front of their living room TV to watch the summer Olympics (which, coincidentally, were taking place only a few miles away), riding mountain bikes around the neighborhood with a half dozen of their friends, or stuffing our faces with hamburgers at the nearby McDonald's, off Ventura. While the son and daughter had been away, I'd managed to pull off a halfway decent impersonation of a sophisticated, thoughtful young man, but after only a few days in the company of teenagers again, I promptly regressed to my loud and obnoxious ways. Gaining the trust of my peers required distance from their parents, but separation from the adults also meant separation from Danny—and I ran into him just one last time, at the dad's medical office, in mid-August. Danny was milling about in the waiting area, cracking up the secretaries, when I waved to him, excited to see him again after many weeks. He nodded, but I got the distinct impression that he didn't recognize me anymore.

And now three years have passed, and I'm a junior at college, in Amherst, Massachusetts (the crummy state school, not the expensive private one); and when the news broke tonight about Danny Kaye, I confided to my friends in the dorm that I'd once eaten barbecued swordfish with him, was his personal guest at a Dodgers game, and all the rest of it. It goes without saying that nobody believed me. They all told me I was full of shit.

I didn't have the strength to argue with them. I've had my issues with embellishment over the years, and even *I* would have to admit that I'm not the most trustworthy person in the world. Chances are, if I'd been in their shoes, I wouldn't have believed me either.

It's still a little hard to talk about, but various aspects of that summer have remained unresolved, three years on. It was my first taste of Los Angeles, and I still haven't quite figured out how to feel about it. A part of me, believe it or not, is somehow convinced that I had an awful time there, that I *hated* the place. It's as if I'm *obligated* to have a negative view of L.A., no matter what.

It would be so easy to make Los Angeles the villain in this story. Believe me, I've tried. The only hitch standing in the way of that is the unfortunate matter of me *adoring* L.A., every damn part of it, from its glaring afternoon sunshine to its palatial swimming pools and spectacular concentration of Famous People (in the Woodland Hills home where I was staying, Lee J. Cobb lived in the house next door until his death, and a member of Supertramp owned the place across the street).

I guess you could say I'm conflicted. That's a word my parents tend to overuse, but, in this case, it might be warranted. Each day I spent in Los Angeles, I wanted nothing more than to fit in with all the moneyed, blissful locals. I was downright giddy the first chance I got to meet a Famous Person, and I'm pretty sure that I've been seeking payback from myself ever since.

Good lord, I get twisted up into knots sometimes. Why can't I just let myself off the hook? Los Angeles hit a nerve with me. I think it revealed a character flaw deep within me that I may never have wanted to discover. And because I'm not remotely strong enough to resist what the city means to me, I pretend to hate it instead, only to feel guilty afterwards because I know that's a lie.

I didn't expect Danny's death to hit me as hard as it did. It turns out that I'm sad as hell. I don't even know precisely why I'm crying, but it's been a few hours and I still can't bring myself to stop. Danny was sweet and funny, and had plenty of magic left. He told dozens of jokes I can no longer remember, invited me to a baseball game at Dodger Stadium, and served me a giant slice of his lemon soufflé.

1987

THE COOKIE THIEF

Alice went around claiming that someone was stealing her food from the dormitory kitchen. This had been going on for quite some time, evidently. The culprit had an affinity for the lactose-free milk Alice kept in the communal refrigerator and, on occasion, would make off with the meats and fish she left out on the counter to defrost.

Word of these infractions hardly penetrated the consciousness of the dorm's two hundred or so coed residents. Among those who lived in the secluded, picturesque three-story brick structure, in the Northeast section of the University of Massachusetts campus, in Amherst, only a dedicated few took the slightest interest in the day-to-day operations of the downstairs kitchen. Students at UMass seemed generally satisfied with the menu options available to them at the school's dining commons, and, besides, the nearest supermarket was far enough away to necessitate a ride on one of the town's dreaded shuttle buses, on which you could never truly escape the smell of vomit. Whatever the reason, fewer than a dozen students in Alice's dormitory availed themselves of the downstairs kitchen.

Alice had a somewhat peculiar reputation among the residents in the building. To the extent that anyone knew about her at all, she was "the girl who hated food." Not *all* food, obviously, but enough of it —ranging from poultry, pasta, soup, pizza, eggs, vegetables, and fruit—to take the fun out of eating. She prepared and ate her meals in isolation, keeping to a rigorous schedule. Her diet consisted of meager portions of either baked potato and pork chop, baked potato and roast beef, or baked potato and fish (but only on Fridays). Every once in a while, she'd substitute the potato for rice pilaf; on those days, the spice packet that was included inside the rice's single-serve cardboard packaging would invariably end up getting tossed in the trash.

It was suggested that Alice's disgust for anything not a potato or a slice of meat was so severe that it might be associated with a medical disorder—but Wilbur had firsthand knowledge of a different category of food Alice could tolerate: cookies. Alice ate cookies. Loads and loads of them, all baked from scratch. Wilbur had on multiple occasions witnessed her spooning out cookie dough in the downstairs kitchen at odd hours of the night.

Alice was a devout Catholic, and each afternoon at precisely four o'clock she'd turn up in the kitchen for another of her spartan meals before dashing off to a nearby chapel just in time for five o'clock Mass. That was about the timeframe when Wilbur and the other members of the Kitchen Crew (admittedly not the most inventive of nicknames) would assemble in the TV lounge adjacent to the kitchen to begin their own dinner preparations.

Wilbur and Derek were first-year members of the Kitchen Crew. An aspiring vegetarian, Derek had recently cancelled his meal plan after growing dissatisfied with, as he put it, its glaring lack of macrobiotic alternatives. For his part, Wilbur had no idea what Derek was talking about. Wilbur didn't have anything against the dining commons food—in fact, he still ate breakfast and lunch there, and would have kept eating dinner there too had he not determined, at the start of the semester, to once and for all teach himself how to cook.

Wilbur had spent the previous two summers working in kitchens around Boston, chopping vegetables and the like. Now, in the waning days of his junior year, he viewed restaurant prep work as a viable Plan B should he fail to snag a respectable job after graduation. No matter how dismal his employment prospects might turn out to be in a year's time, Wilbur felt confident he could always earn a living by working in restaurants until something better came along.

On his first chance to stock up on groceries, Wilbur bought curry paste, ginger root, smoked paprika, black peppercorns, and *herbes de Provence*. He was at the very early stages of his culinary journey and still had a lot of catching up to do. Once, when Derek arrived late to dinner and remarked that the whole kitchen smelled of cardamom, Wilbur responded: "Sure, if you say so."

Wilbur was an English major, but was suffering of late from nagging second thoughts. No matter which requisite course he was forced to endure, he couldn't seem to escape some combination of Virginia Woolf, Nathaniel Hawthorne, or Herman Melville—and he was getting pretty damned tired of it. During a routine check-in with his academic advisor, Wilbur confided that he wasn't taking pleasure in the novels that comprised his curricula—essential works regarded among the finest literary achievements of the Western canon—and his advisor replied without a trace of irony that perhaps Wilbur had picked the wrong major.

But Wilbur didn't hate *all* books, just the ones assigned to him by his professors. He became expert at pairing each purported masterwork with an offbeat title of his own choosing, balancing every dreary so-called classic with something far less irritating or convoluted. He was naturally drawn to modern American authors who avoided fancy words and flowery prose. Kurt Vonnegut was a personal favorite, but the professors in Wilbur's English department deemed Vonnegut's minimalist, satiric style unworthy of scholarly analysis. And so, whenever Wilbur was about to crack open another Important Novel for a course such as Romanticism, Realism, Practical Criticism, or Major British Writers, he already knew at the outset that he was going to hate it and have a hell of a time getting through it.

His professors didn't seem to notice or care that they were all living eight decades into a new century; with each passing semester, it appeared increasingly unlikely that Wilbur would get assigned anything published by an American author after "Huckleberry Finn." As a practical matter, this meant having to discover certain authors on his own. Nathanael West and Sherwood Anderson were recent finds, but even established giants such as Fitzgerald and Hemingway were judged to be of insufficient literary import to warrant consideration by his professors (exceptions would now and again be made for William Faulkner, who seemed to exist in a category all his own—but this did Wilbur no favors). A similar arrangement appeared to exist outside the classroom as well: judging from the inadequate selection of modern

American novels housed inside the university's imposing library tower, little of note was published in the second half of the 20th century anyway. To get his hands on the kind of fiction that reminded Wilbur why he wanted to be an English major in the first place, he needed to scour the paperback aisles of used bookstores in Amherst Center, where every so often he'd unearth just the sort of hidden gem his professors seemed all too eager to dismiss. What a perfect day it turned out to be when, quite by accident, he came across a collection of short stories by Bruce Jay Friedman.

* * * *

In the springtime, on Good Friday, Alice returned home to Central Massachusetts to attend services at her family's church. Derek, also Catholic, returned home to attend services at *his* family's church as well. It turned out that a preponderance of the students in Wilbur's dorm were Catholic (who knew?) and were planning to celebrate Easter in their hometown churches. But Wilbur was Jewish, and had, in fact, visited his parents earlier in the month for mandatory attendance at his family's Passover Seder (this year, Passover came and went earlier than usual, due to the vagaries of the Jewish calendar), so, as far as he was concerned, he had neither the rationale nor the appetite to go back home anytime soon.

Sunday was Easter, of course, but Monday was also a holiday—Patriots' Day—albeit one observed primarily in Massachusetts. This made for a rare four-day weekend, and the campus was emptying out fast. Even Wilbur's roommate, Chuck, who hated his parents and had no intention of getting within ten miles of a church service, figured he might as well go home too. At most, fewer than a dozen students chose to remain in the dorm over the long holiday weekend, leaving Wilbur almost perfectly alone.

On Friday afternoon, at his favorite used bookstore, he snagged a dog-eared copy of William Goldman's "The Temple of Gold" and dove right into it, in spite of the fact that his essay on "The Scarlet Letter" was due after the long weekend and he wasn't yet halfway through it. That evening, he considered catching a double feature at the revival movie theater in town, but after it was dark outside and the dorm got dead quiet, he chose to stay in and relax instead. The same thing happened Saturday night: he stayed in and relaxed. When a student he barely knew sat down next to him in the otherwise empty TV lounge to watch a sitcom, Wilbur said to him, "you Jewish?" and the guy said, "yeah," and Wilbur said, "yeah, me too."

On Easter Sunday, as the sun peered out from behind ominous clouds, Wilbur brought the Goldman and the Hawthorne with him to the grassy incline overlooking the Campus Pond. He tore through the

Goldman but struggled to get past a single paragraph of the Hawthorne, before closing his eyes and drifting off to sleep.

Wilbur didn't notice the plate of cookies resting atop the communal refrigerator in the downstairs kitchen until late Sunday evening. He had little reason to look in that direction at all, having recently purchased a mini-fridge for his dorm room. Moreover, he'd heard rumblings about Alice's food getting stolen from the communal refrigerator downstairs and wanted no part of that drama.

Wilbur's room was two flights up, and each evening he'd gather an array of refrigerated ingredients to bring downstairs with him when it came time to cook his dinner (he kept his nonperishable items stored in a locked cabinet in the kitchen). On this particular Sunday night, the recipe he was following called for butter, and it was the one ingredient he'd failed to account for. Rather than hike up all those steps for a measly tablespoon of butter, he opened the refrigerator, found someone else's stick, and helped himself to the precise amount needed. That's when he spotted the plate of cookies above the fridge, covered by a long sheet of plastic-wrap, and they were plump, gorgeous chocolate chip tollhouses with chopped walnuts, or possibly pecans, or maybe they were macadamias? Whatever was in them, Wilbur knew right away these were Alice's cookies.

He finished preparing his dinner and ate it while watching TV in the adjacent lounge; afterwards, for dessert, he carefully lifted the plastic-wrap to snag one of Alice's creations. *Goddamit, that was delicious,* he thought to himself (macadamias, it turned out); *no wonder she eats so many of these.* It required tremendous willpower on his part to resist grabbing a second cookie. After washing and putting away his dishes, he retreated upstairs to take another crack at "The Scarlet Letter," but lost focus straightaway and fell asleep in his clothes.

It was midnight when he awoke next, cringing in pain from a mysterious, searing spasm that seemed to emanate from his stomach. Racing to the bathroom, he sat on the cleanest toilet he could find without a moment to spare; the waves of diarrhea he endured over the next half hour were too ghastly for words. Rinsing his hands at the sink in the aftermath, he naively tricked himself into believing the worst was over, before whipping around and going through the same ordeal all over again. *It must have been something I ate,* he guessed.

He felt moderately less nauseous on Patriots' Day, and passed the time on a couch in the TV lounge, trying once more to finish "The Scarlet Letter." As dusk approached, whatever was going on inside his stomach had mostly run its course. After his second or third visit to a toilet that day, he lingered at the bathroom mirror to pop a pimple on his forehead, a diversion that seemed oddly comforting under the circumstances.

By nightfall, his appetite regained, he stepped into the kitchen for the first time in twenty-four hours to prepare something light to eat. Glancing at the plate of cookies on top of the refrigerator, he saw that they'd all been eaten—save a few broken pieces scattered around the edges of the dish. Momentarily tempted, he avoided these remaining crumbs; his stomach hadn't fully settled down yet, and it was hard enough getting through half a turkey sandwich.

Students began to trickle back into the dorm after dark. Wilbur and Chuck sat on the floor in their room, drinking beer out of cans.

"It's good to see people again," Wilbur said.

"You won't say that tomorrow," Chuck cautioned him.

"I know, but it feels good to miss 'em anyway, even if I'll hate 'em tomorrow."

They downed one can after another as neighbors dropped in to share anecdotes, some interesting, some not, from their long weekends at home. Frank, who lived across the hall, recounted an episode during Easter services at his church that had made him feel a bit uncomfortable. A special booklet was handed out to his congregation with a passage in it that resembled a scene from a play rather than a customary benediction. The priest assigned three or four congregants roles as witnesses to the crucifixion, with the priest taking the part of Pontius Pilate for himself (Jesus didn't have any lines, so no one had to play Him).

As the scene reached its dramatic crescendo, the full congregation was eventually prompted to speak in unison—and this was the part that had made Frank feel a bit uncomfortable. Whenever Pontius Pilate put Jesus's fate in the hands of the mob, the cue for the congregants to shout "crucify him!" wasn't *Crowd* or *Onlookers* or *Assembly*—it was *Jews*.

"I hate that story," Wilbur said. "It's gross."

"Maybe the Jews really did kill Christ," Chuck said, and Wilbur tossed at empty beer can at him.

"Fine, but maybe they could've tried harder to save Him," Chuck continued. "Maybe they could've picked one of the other guys to nail to the cross instead, and then maybe Christians wouldn't hate Jews so much."

"Give me a break," Wilbur said. "Why should Jews get the blame for choosing one man to die over another? If crucifixion is supposedly so awful and gruesome, what difference should it make who got picked? And the Jews weren't the people in charge, now were they? It was the Romans who carried out the whole bloody mess—and quite ruthlessly, I might add. They *invented* the damn torture device that Jesus hung on. The Jews didn't have anything to do with *that*. And besides, where would Christianity be today if the mob had told

Pilate to kill one of those other guys instead? Think about it: Here was this brand new offshoot of Judaism, explicitly promising to improve on the previous version, and, in their *most important story,* they lay the blame for killing their Savior on the one religion they just so happened to be setting out to replace. Doesn't that seem a bit convenient to you?"

"I don't know, Wilbur," Chuck said. "Don't worry so much about it."

* * * *

The next day, Alice wrote a note and taped it to a wall in the TV lounge next door to the kitchen. The note read: "I hope the people who stole my cookies over the weekend are proud of themselves. I mixed two entire cartons of ex-lax into the batter, so for your sake, I hope they were delicious."

When Wilbur read the note, he was too dumbstruck to have any sort of meaningful reaction, and instead raced upstairs to share the news with Derek and Chuck.

"What a *bitch*," Derek said.

"What a *hypocrite*," Chuck said.

"She should get in *serious trouble* for this," Derek said.

"She should get *kicked out of the dorm* for this," Chuck said.

"So, did you get diarrhea?" Derek asked.

"Yeah, did you get the shits?" Chuck asked.

"Damn right I got the shits!" Wilbur yelled back at them. "I ate one stupid cookie, got sick as hell, and had no idea why—and now I'm super pissed off!"

Here's where Wilbur may have miscalculated: swayed perhaps by a sudden burst of righteous indignation, he marched straight over to Alice's room and banged on her door. When she opened it, he admitted right off the bat that he'd eaten one of her cookies over the weekend and had gotten sick from it.

"Well, if you weren't such a lowdown dirty thief," Alice shrieked, "stealing other people's food all the time, maybe this wouldn't have happened to you. It serves you right for taking what isn't yours, so I'm glad you got sick, because at least now I know who the goddamned thief is!" And then she slammed the door in Wilbur's face.

Wilbur couldn't believe it. Was Alice blaming him for stealing her food, *all* her food, all the food that had ever been taken from her, just because he ate one lousy cookie? To make matters worse, he still needed to pull an all-nighter if he was going to have any chance of finishing "The Scarlet Letter" and banging out an essay on Hawthorne's use of ambiguity by Wednesday afternoon. Near 4:00 a.m., still unable to get through the last hundred pages of the book, he threw in the towel, deciding his only option was to limit his essay to the earlier parts of the novel and hope the teacher didn't notice.

The following night, as he was about to start cooking dinner in the dorm kitchen, two of Alice's friends ambushed him in front of a sizable crowd in the TV lounge and accused him of stealing Alice's food. Wilbur tried to defend himself, but one of the girls said, "well, you ate a cookie, didn't you?" and Wilbur said, "yeah, I ate a cookie, so what?" and she said, "well, that's stealing," and Wilbur said, "what about what Alice did, what about poisoning the cookies?" and the girl said, "it wasn't poison because it didn't kill you," and Wilbur said, "yeah, but it made me sick and I had a horrible reaction to it," and so on.

Wilbur ended up being the only person in the dorm willing to admit to eating one of Alice's poisoned cookies, and that was bad enough. Having to defend himself against accusations that he was also guilty of stealing her frozen meats, fish, and lactose-free milk was no picnic either. And getting humiliated by Alice's rowdy friends in the crowded TV lounge was surely a low point. But the worst moment of all came the very next day, when Wilbur discovered yet another note someone had posted in the TV lounge. This note was addressed specifically to him, and it read: "Wilbur, you dirty Jew, stop stealing other people's food." It was unsigned.

Wilbur knew a guy who lived at the other end of his floor who was planning to apply to law school, so he rushed over to the guy's room and related the entire sequence of events to see what recourse he might have against Alice.

"Well, I guess it could be viewed as entrapment," the guy planning to apply to law school said. "That is, a cop can't sell drugs to someone and then turn around and arrest him for buying those drugs."

"He can't?"

"No, that's illegal. At least I'm pretty sure it is. And anyway, Alice had no intention of eating those cookies or sharing them with her friends. You can't put something out in public, knowing it will get stolen, in fact *counting* on it getting stolen, then complain afterwards when it's taken. Now that I think about it, she probably warned certain people *in advance* to stay away from those cookies, giving them prior knowledge of the scheme—the literal definition of a criminal conspiracy. Every person she warned to stay away from those cookies might also be an accomplice after the fact, though that might be harder to prove. I'd need to look into that. But let's not forget: Alice put those cookies out knowing full well people would get sick, which demonstrates a clear malicious intent on her part. It's a bit of a gray area, but I think you may have a case."

"Perfect," Wilbur said. "I'm gonna use all of that."

So he marched over to Alice's room a second time and banged on her door yet again to repeat everything he'd just learned from the guy who was planning to apply to law school. "Leave it to a Jew to quote the law," Alice shot back, and that was about the moment Wilbur understood he wouldn't be coming out ahead on this one.

1987

STRICTLY SPEAKING

George and Paula lived next door to each other in a twelve-story apartment building on the corner of 53rd and 9th Avenue, a single, poorly insulated wall on either side of their bedrooms the only barrier keeping them apart. Paula moved in first and had been there hardly a month when, without warning, the elderly Filipino lady in the adjacent unit dropped dead and George swooped in. A realtor brought him around to have a look at the place while the dead woman's belongings were still in it; by week's end, George and one of his co-workers rode the building's rickety elevator up and down as many times as it took to transport his sofa, television, mattress, and desk.

George was fond of saying that he was a sous-chef at a failing midtown Italian restaurant, but "glorified prep cook" was closer to the truth. He chopped vegetables. Paula worked as a secretary at a law firm near Rockefeller Plaza, and, like George, was not averse to exaggerating her job title from time to time, bumping herself up to paralegal should anyone bother to ask what she did for a living. Still, in each of their hearts, they were neither prep cook/sous-chef nor secretary/paralegal. George was a novelist, Paula an actress. Or, to put it more precisely, that was how they defined themselves.

Despite her best efforts, Paula hadn't yet made a dent in theatrical circles on or off Broadway; nonetheless, she had no intention of giving up on her dreams any time soon. Lacking representation, she kept a watchful eye out for open casting calls featured in the classified section of *Backstage* magazine, booking gigs now and again on local commercials for used cars or king-sized mattresses. The occasion of her twenty-second birthday, celebrated with a small group of secretaries from her office, also marked her fourth anniversary in New York—she'd caught a bus to Port Authority on the day she'd turned eighteen.

George, a year older than Paula, switched off his personal computer one Sunday morning in early June after spending the previous ten hours moving commas around in his troublesome novel, "Self-Assertiveness in the Suicidal Male" (it was a working title and he was open to changing it). By daybreak, he was a wreck. He grabbed his windbreaker and headed out for a coffee at the very instant Paula was returning home from an all-night party at a downtown loft.

They brushed against each other as she was stepping off the elevator and he was stepping on—an event of such glaring insignificance that it could hardly be mistaken for a "meet-cute" moment from one of those run-of-the-mill romantic comedies out of Hollywood.

Sharing similar start-times at each of their jobs (prep cooks are among the first staff to arrive at most restaurants), George and Paula would often set off for work within minutes of the other. Polite "hellos" and varied pleasantries during all-too-brief elevator rides extended from the lobby to the pavement outside their building, until, after a time, they found they could get as far as a newspaper stand and the French bakery on 7th, where they would each order a large black coffee before heading off in opposite directions. One innocuous exchange led to the next, until, without premeditation, they went from lingering together at their mailboxes—comparing junk mail and bills—to impromptu strolls around the neighborhood without any set destination in mind. One radiant spring morning, both of them sleeping in, Paula knocked on George's door and slipped a note underneath it before scurrying back to her apartment. The note read: "Please join me for more caffeine than usual," which George took to mean that their smalltalk phase had finally come to an end.

"What are you writing about?" she asked him that morning at the French bakery.

"I can't seem to write about anything lately," George confessed. "Whenever I try, all that comes out are scenes with vegetables."

"Come on, I don't believe you."

"I swear it's true. Last night I wrote about a character who dreams he's surrounded by parsley. Other vegetables too. Parsley, celery, cucumbers, and eggplant."

"What a coincidence—that happens to be my favorite Simon & Garfunkel song," she joked, before belting out the chorus with revised lyrics.

George was lying, sort of. While it was true that there was a character in his novel who dreams of being surrounded by vegetables, what George failed to mention to Paula was that the individual in question—a twenty-three year old malcontent named Jeff—was in fact the hero and narrator of his sprawling, aforementioned novel, "Self-Assertiveness in the Suicidal Male." The book, which even George might concede was turning into an unmitigated fiasco, documents the psychological deterioration of a young writer incapable of bouncing back from a painful breakup.

Jeff, the protagonist in George's novel, takes a job chopping vegetables at an Italian restaurant while staying up late most nights to work on his dark, excessively verbose novel about a failed relationship. Out of the blue, Jodie, Jeff's ex-girlfriend, invites him to lunch, causing Jeff to speculate that perhaps she's had a change of heart and wishes to reconcile. As it happens, her motivation is simply to inform him that she's gotten engaged and plans to move to a split-level house in New Jersey with her fiancé. Upon hearing the news, Jeff, now more despondent than ever, settles on a plan to commit suicide with cyanide-laced cigarettes.

George had yet to tackle this rather grim section of his novel, but the idea was to have Jeff somehow misplace his poisoned cigarettes and, in the remaining chapters, obsess over the possibility that some unfortunate soul might stumble upon them by chance, light one up, and die.

George, much like his fictional counterpart, was recovering from a recent breakup, although he would have bristled at any suggestion his work was somehow autobiographical. For starters, George's ex-girlfriend's name was Judy, not Jodie. Also, it should be noted, George's separation from Judy wasn't nearly as traumatic as the one depicted in his book: after Judy, George's ex, got accepted into the graduate linguistics program at Boston University, she and George agreed to end their three-month long relationship on the spot. Even so, George opted not to share these plot details with Paula. He didn't want her to think he was crazy.

In July, when George had a night off from the restaurant, he somehow found the nerve to ask Paula out on a date. She leapt at the chance, suggesting a Jean-Luc Godard double feature that was playing at her favorite revival cinema in the West Village. On their way back uptown, sometime around midnight, they popped into a deli for cigarettes, where Paula spotted a pinball machine in the corner of the store and immediately began to play. Feeling emboldened—as if he'd stepped into a French New Wave movie—George crept up behind Paula to deposit a lit cigarette between her lips. Paula carried on with her game without skipping a beat, the cigarette bobbing up and down in her mouth as she manipulated both flippers with surprising dexterity.

Impressed by her technique, George leaned in for a closer look, which was the exact moment he noticed for the first time a rather sizable diamond ring on her left hand.

"Hey, what's the deal with that giant rock on your finger?" he asked her.

"What about it?" she replied, without looking up from her game.

"Well, shit. Is it connected to your love life in some way I should know about?" He finally got around to lighting his own cigarette.

"I suppose so," she said, not volunteering more information than that.

Another minute passed, and George couldn't take the suspense any longer. "Jesus, Paula, are you getting married, or what?"

"I'm engaged, if you must know. He's coming to town on Sunday, as a matter of fact, to spend the afternoon. Now let me finish my game, will ya?"

It was the second weekend in July and New York was already blistering hot. George occupied himself on the worst Sunday of his life with *The New York Times* crossword puzzle and an Elvis Presley movie marathon on TV. The bedroom wall he shared with Paula could just as easily have been constructed out of tissue paper: one minute, he could hear Paula wheezing as if she were having an asthma attack, the next she'd be panting, moaning, grunting, and God knows what else. Her fiancé never made a sound. Once it became clear that Elvis's bad acting wasn't up to the task of drowning out Paula's heavy breathing, George turned the volume all the way down on his set to listen exclusively to her.

When dusk approached, an uncharacteristic silence ensued, interrupted only by the creaking of Paula's front door as it opened. The next sound George heard was the echo of an emphatic kiss that ricocheted down the corridor. Then, farther away still, the piercing sound of the elevator's chime.

* * * *

Cyanide can be obtained in liquid or gaseous forms. George was trying to determine how Jeff, his protagonist, could acquire the poison. You can't just walk into a pharmacy and grab it off the shelf in the cyanide aisle, George knew. And even if Jeff could get his hands on it, what form would it be in, and how would he go about injecting it into the cigarettes? George took a drag off his own cigarette, paying close attention to the sound of the paper as it burned. His mind circled back to Paula, who was doubtless passed out from an extended afternoon of vigorous fucking. *Enough*, he chided himself, turning his attention once more to cyanide.

A solution presented itself courtesy of the high school chemistry textbook he kept around for research, however infrequent. George identified a type of hard plastic commonly found in household items that, when melted, released cyanide gas. All Jeff would need to do is inject a few drops of melted plastic into his cigarettes, and then, when he was ready to kill himself, lie back in his most comfortable chair and smoke away the remaining minutes of his life. The injected plastic would melt yet again, releasing lethal doses of cyanide into his lungs along with the usual quantities of tar and nicotine for good measure. Assuming George wasn't misreading the data in his dog-eared chemistry book, his hero would stop breathing by his third or fourth cigarette.

George wrote throughout the night. "I sit alone preparing for my imminent departure. I've gone through two packs—one I've smoked (there's scarcely been a moment all night when I didn't have a cigarette in my mouth), the other I've gladly sacrificed to experimentation. At first, I assumed any plastic would do, and broke off pieces from the wing of an old model airplane. But those fragments were a dark grey and remained visible through the cigarette paper, and that wouldn't do. I needed to avoid *seeing* the poison as I smoked myself into oblivion. Instead, I crushed an old cassette tape case into tiny pieces (the tape was "Greetings from Asbury Park," for whatever it's worth), which, when melted, looked perfectly transparent. The trickiest part, it turned out, was getting the melted plastic injected into the cigarettes before it hardened again in the syringe."

It was Paula's idea to see a *Shakespeare in the Park* production of "Twelfth Night" one August evening as dark storm clouds rolled through Central Park. Predicted showers held off until the very end of the play, when, as the cast converged at center stage to sing what turned out to be a comically appropriate rendition of "The Wind and the Rain," the skies opened overhead, drenching actors and audience alike.

Holding their Playbills above them like makeshift umbrellas, neither George nor Paula could stop laughing. Paula's makeup ran down her face as her cashmere sweater clung to her breasts. George couldn't take his eyes off her. They dashed through the pouring rain like characters in a Woody Allen movie before slipping into the first bar they passed for a round of Stoli vodka tonics. Crammed together in a corner booth, a flickering candle their only source of light, Paula announced her intention to rush outside and splash around in puddles as soon as she finished her drink. George pleaded with her to wait out the storm. Every so often, a drop of water would fall from her hair and land gently in her vodka tonic.

Several rounds later—George lost count—dizzy from cigarettes and alcohol, they held a frenzied, rousing discussion about love, lust, and heartache with an older, considerably more sophisticated couple in the next booth. Paula introduced George as her "lover," and, to prove it, she nibbled on his ear. George, blushing, began to shiver uncontrollably. At one point, he let his arm drop and it landed on Paula's knee, where he left it for so long that his elbow locked up. During the cab ride home, Paula, exhausted, lay her head on George's still damp shoulder. He was dying to kiss her, and twice, he almost did; but as they faced their respective apartment doors, each of them fumbling for the key, George could sense that the spell they'd been under for much of the night had finally started to wear off.

In the weeks that followed, George saw more and more of Paula. She'd knock three times on their common bedroom wall, and he'd knock three times back. Sometimes, instead of knocking, she'd just yell, "Hey, George!" and he'd open his front door and stick his head into the hallway, turning to his left, as Paula performed the same maneuver, only turning to her right.

They took to watching TV in her apartment on the nights when George wasn't at work. Once, she offered to give him a back rub, and he proceeded to cozy up beside her on the couch, sitting directly on top of fashion magazines and folded laundry. By the time she was through massaging his neck and shoulders, he could've sworn it was all a dream. "Come on," she pleaded with him, "it's my turn," so they switched places —but George was unable to get past the idea that his hands were truly resting on Paula's upper torso, and forgot all about the massage. He might have stayed that way for another hour or so had she not spoken up. "A little harder, okay?" she whispered, snapping him out of his trance.

Later that same week, Paula ditched work early to catch the last rays of the sun, and ran into George at the mailboxes downstairs. Within minutes, they'd each changed into seldom worn bathing suits and were laying on towels twelve stories above the city, chain-smoking his Camels. Paula wore a light blue bikini, and it was the most George had ever seen of her pale, skinny frame. It felt as if he were breaking some kind of law just by looking at her.

Paula had a lot on her mind that day—she was more talkative than usual—but George found it difficult to concentrate on what she was saying and only heard fragments: "There's an off-off-Broadway production in the works I'm gonna audition for...he's not coming 'til Sunday again...it's kind of a Sam Shepard knock-off, so how bad can it be?...why isn't he coming 'til Sunday?...if I get the part, things will need to change, the marriage can wait...the role I'm best suited for is the daughter, she's young and poor and sassy...God, I'm so sick and tired of my fiancé...I'm gonna need a Southern accent, but I should be able to fake that...all this wedding talk is getting out of hand...I have dreams, dammit! Just like you, George, I have dreams...where do you want to eat Chinese food tonight?"

George stole glances from behind his knock-off Ray-Bans, his indiscretion growing more apparent by the minute. After a time, Paula wrapped herself in an oversized shawl and repositioned her ridiculous straw hat until it covered most of her face.

* * * *

He awoke to a series of loud knocks on the bedroom wall they shared, just before dawn.

"Can you hear me?" she cried out, her voice trembling.

"Yes."

"I can't sleep, obviously," she laughed—or was it a sob? "Can I come over?"

Paula entered his living room wearing cut-off shorts and a T-shirt that stopped just short of her waist. He offered her a glass of milk which she proceeded to consume in two enormous gulps an instant before she started to cry. Intermittent tears escaped from the corners of her eyes every couple of seconds, and George had no idea what to do about it. He thought of hugging her but passed her a box of Kleenex instead.

Her tears only increased as she positioned herself on his couch, her elbows now resting on the tops of her knees as her hands covered her face. He sat as far away from her as possible, on the wobbly three-legged stool he kept off to one side of the room, and watched as she continued to sob into her hands. He waited. When he saw her face again, it was as if she were coming up for air: her chest rose and fell with each deep breath.

"You wanna talk about it?" he asked, after her breathing slowed.

"It's better if I don't," she said. The whites of her eyes had transformed into a blur of bright pink.

"Could this have anything to do with your fiancé?"

"Your powers of perception are legendary, George."

They kept silent a moment longer, until she blurted out: "He's such a fucking *asshole!*"

"What?"

"I hate him so fucking much! I wish I'd never laid eyes on him! He's cruel, heartless, compassionless, and he knows nothing about art or culture or *anything.* He's entirely unromantic. He's a contract lawyer for a shoe company, for Chrissakes! He's always complaining about how much he hates the city. Can you believe it, George? *This* city! He thinks it's *filthy*. He wants me to move to Connecticut. *Connecticut!* I get so furious sometimes. He couldn't care less about my dreams. I doubt it would bother him one bit if I never acted again!"

George was too stunned to come up with anything resembling a thoughtful response.

"I'm awfully sorry, George" she continued. "I didn't mean to dump this on you. I get so lonely, that's all. I had to talk to you tonight, to be with you." She paused briefly to blow her nose. "I have *needs*, George. I have desires. He's away. He's *always* away. And when he's here, I assume everything will be okay if we go to bed. So we do. We fuck. Sometimes we're so loud, I'm afraid you'll hear us through the bedroom wall." She paused to intercept a tear as it slid down her cheek. "But that's all we do. We don't talk. We don't laugh. We don't cry —"

"Listen, Paula —"

"We just *fuck!* I don't know what to do anymore. How am I supposed to marry a man I don't love?"

"I understand, Paula, and —"

"George! George! I'm scared! I feel as if I'm about to make a catastrophic mistake, and there's not a thing in the world I can do to stop it!"

"*Please!*" he shouted, without any idea how he might finish his sentence. She tugged on her shirt. "Please," he repeated, much softer this time, "you're forgetting about me. You're forgetting how I fit in. I've never needed anyone as much as I need you. Right now, with you sitting here, on my sofa, I'm...I'm going out of my mind. And when I'm not with you, or worse, when you're sleeping with—ah dammit, I can't remember his *name*—I just want to kill myself. I *love* you, Paula. Whether or not you want to hear it, I'm in love with you."

"Oh *God!*" she shrieked, her face disappearing once again into the palms of her hands. He turned away to light a cigarette, thinking, *that's it, I did it, it's over, she hates me.*

"This is insane," Paula said. "This is torture. You're a nice boy, George, and you can find plenty of girls. What do you want with a girl like me?"

He felt a sudden urge to jam his cigarette into his forehead, burning a hole right through his skull and into his brain. By the time he was able to look at her again, she wasn't crying anymore, her eyes had magically reverted to their unblemished state, her hair was tucked neatly behind her ears, and both her bare feet were touching the floor.

Just as he was about to open his mouth to speak— what he might've said to her at that moment is anyone's guess—Paula hopped off the sofa, thanked him for the glass of milk, and marched straight out of his apartment.

They had plans to spend an evening together later in the week, but Paula cancelled at the last minute, mentioning something about "getting into the zone" for her upcoming audition. The following week, he figured he'd save her the trouble of inventing another excuse and let it slip that nothing good was playing at the revival cinemas. Crossing paths at the mailboxes in late August, Paula remarked almost as an afterthought that her fiancé had made an offer on an adorable three bedroom ranch-style house he'd been eyeing in Stamford.

George ran into her one last time, on the elevator. He hardly got a word in. She talked a mile a minute about the lavish resort in the Bahamas where she and her fiancé planned to spend their honeymoon, the high-priced salon where she was getting her hair styled and braided before the wedding, whether or not it was too late to have her dress altered to make it sleeveless, and what to do with the hideous set of gold-plated dinnerware promised to her by a distant relative in Minneapolis. At one point, George tried asking about the play, but she cut him off with a wave of her hand and told him she'd skipped the audition, never stood a chance of landing that part anyway. On a muggy September afternoon, her fiancé and a few of his friends pulled up to the building in a rented van, and, by nightfall, Paula was gone.

1988

LAST STOP ON THE GRAVY TRAIN

The group of friends Sam hung around with in high school were scattered across the country now, preparing for careers in law, finance, medicine, and engineering; but Sam had no interest in any of those things. Briefly, as a boy, he'd fantasied about joining the professional tennis circuit when he grew up, until the other kids at his summer camp spelled out to him in no uncertain terms that he stunk at tennis and had better get used to watching matches on TV. Sam took that news in stride, figured none of those jerks would end up going pro either. *No big deal*, he thought, *I'll just find something else to do.*

In those days, children were rarely asked what they wanted to *do* when they grew up. That sort of specificity was frowned upon. Rather, the question was framed in existential terms: what do you want to *be*? It was a subtle distinction, but, to Sam, it made all the difference. Planning his future around ways to earn a living was one thing, but what command could he ever manage over his *being?*

What do you want to be when you grow up, Sam? What do you want to *be?*

To help him arrive at an answer, he made lists. At first, he embraced the distinction between everyday run-of-the-mill job titles and something that might satisfy the requirements of a meaningful goal. Early on, for instance, "happy" routinely landed at the top of his list—as in, "I want to be *happy* when I grow up." This held until about the fifth grade, when Sam, for varied and complex reasons, concluded that happiness was for suckers.

Fine. He could live without happiness (it's not as if his world was overflowing with it to begin with). He would just need to find another worthy goal to aspire to.

Major League shortstop. Brain surgeon. Fireman. Astronaut. President of the United States. Zookeeper. Environmental activist. News anchor. Olympic athlete. Top-rated chef. Civil rights attorney. Airline pilot. Pulitzer Prize-winning journalist. Scuba diver. Police detective. Veterinarian.

He'd memorized this list by the time he started junior high, intent on having answers at the ready should anyone happen to inquire. Interestingly, he never bothered to take the extra step of writing any of it down. Each time he thought about generating a tangible record of the list that could exist outside his mind, he determined there was simply no need: he knew its contents by heart, so what would be the point? In his imagination, he'd already inscribed it in tiny block lettering on a sheet of lined paper that he folded up afterwards into a plump little square and carried around with him in his back pocket.

Throughout his adolescence, Sam kept learning the hard way that yet another entry on his list would have to get crossed out, one aspirational goal at a time. Nope, sorry kid, you haven't got the chops for that, you wouldn't be any good at it. No, no, not *that* one either —that field is entirely out of the question. And please forget about that other thing too, will you, because the competition is ferocious and you haven't got a prayer.

At some point it dawned on Sam that there wasn't anything left on his list that remained realistically within his grasp. All the options had been crossed out. The folded up square of paper (still imaginary) he carried around in his back pocket had gone through the wash by accident so many times that it had finally been turned to dust.

By the time he reached seventeen, an ever-shrinking catalog of dream jobs was the least of his concerns: Sam's equilibrium had all but disintegrated too. He kept mostly to himself in high school, reading comic books or watching old movies on his family's basement TV. His mother was stuck in a grievance and disapproval loop; everything upset her, everyone was out to get her.

"Damned if I do, damned if I don't," she'd recite like a mantra, regardless of circumstance. Sam's father had his own baggage, couldn't control his temper. He'd scream at the top of his lungs, smashing dishes, punching walls (Sam feared his father might drop dead from a heart attack at any moment). Meanwhile, his older brother Andy had unexpectedly joined the Army Reserve, disappearing from Sam's life for weeks at a time.

A stabilizing force during those messy years was photography. It may have been the only thing that kept him from losing his mind. All the same, Sam never regarded photography as anything other than a hobby, a way to let off steam. After all, how would one go about earning a living as a photographer? Was that even a real job?

When it came time to choosing which colleges to apply to, art school never stood a chance. He'd pursue a bachelor's degree in something practical instead— history, or maybe economics. Anything but the arts. Art school was for weirdos. Spoiled rich kids went to art school. Anti-social, drug addicted rich kids. Even if a college put the word *fine* in front of it to lend their degree some badly needed legitimacy, it was still a scam.

But that was last year. Now, Sam knew better.

His freshman year at Boston University had been a total disaster: he'd failed three classes his first semester and four the next, was essentially flunking out as early as Passover, in April. He withdrew of his own accord before the end of the term—the face-saving equivalent of quitting your job just as you're about to get fired.

In the immediate aftermath of his flame-out from B.U., the instinct to photograph the world around him took hold once more. Sadly, he no longer owned a camera (long story), leaving him little choice but to push those impulses off to the side. He was penniless, but moving back home with his parents was hardly an option: they had practically disowned him. With expenses mounting, he took a job washing dishes at a Brookline Village seafood restaurant, scarcely earning enough at the end of each week to afford the lease on the shittiest apartment he could find. Each time he put on an apron, he felt as if he were performing a kind of penance. *Photography will have to wait,* he told himself while scrubbing burnt fish skins from stainless steel frying pans. Still, that didn't quite explain what compelled him to steal a six-pack of Heineken from the restaurant's walk-in refrigerator when there were a handful of witnesses around.

His subsequent firing from his *next* job, working in the stock room of a video store on Commonwealth Avenue, was, as far as he was concerned, entirely unjustified; all he did was let his old high school buddies Davis and Perry buy a couple of crappy movies using his thirty percent employee discount.

Needless to say, Sam's sudden flurry of irresponsible behavior didn't sit well with his parents, who were already livid that he'd poured sixteen thousand dollars of their hard-earned savings down the drain. They gave him the cold-shoulder throughout much of that summer, refusing to speak with him even after he'd dropped off a contrite card on their wedding anniversary and another on his mother's birthday—and his abrupt dismissals from two low-paying jobs weren't helping matters. He'd been operating under the assumption that, sooner or later, they'd *have* to forgive him, as long as he kept the apologies coming. But an August heatwave brought with it no softening of their position, and a new strategy seemed in order.

He turned up at their Newton Centre house uninvited, refusing to budge until they consented to a discussion about his future. Seated around their kitchen table, Sam couldn't shake the impression that he'd thrown himself at the mercy of the court. He understood precisely what he was up against: a scolding of historic proportions, a lecture to end all lectures, etc. But he was willing to endure just about anything if it got him out of the hole he'd dug for himself.

The evening didn't go as expected. The scolding he'd anticipated turned out to be relatively mild, the lecture brief and painless. What they proposed instead took Sam altogether by surprise.

One class. They'd pay for one class.

Choose wisely, his mother cautioned, *as if the rest of your life depends on it.*

Don't screw this up, his father warned, less diplomatically, *'cause there won't be anymore goddamned bailouts after this one.*

They pleaded with Sam not to underestimate the gravity of his situation. *Please understand, Sam. We're not kidding around this time. This is the last stop on the gravy train.*

It took Sam fewer than five minutes to announce his decision, a delay that had more to do with waiting for his father to return from the bathroom than any requirement on Sam's part to deliberate. Impulsive by nature, Sam knew right off the bat which class he wanted to take, and exactly where he wanted to take it.

"Jesus fucking Christ," his father groaned when learning of Sam's intentions. "I should've seen *that* coming."

* * * *

The School of the Museum of Fine Arts, or The Museum School, as it was commonly referred to, had the most highly regarded photography program in all of Boston. Sam's high school photography teacher had received his fine arts degree from there, and Sam was on friendly terms with a few classmates from Newton South who were currently enrolled at the college as undergraduates. In spite of the fact that the fall semester was about to get underway, Sam felt confident that, with a referral from his former teacher and a tuition check from his parents, he could audit Intermediate Photography for the rest of the term before having to officially enroll at the college as a full-time student.

Undergrads at The Museum School received unfettered access to the school's darkrooms and facilities, and could borrow additional equipment, such as lenses and tripods, to complete their assignments. But, as Sam was acutely aware, getting worthwhile results from a school-issued camera was an entirely different matter. No self-respecting photography student would ever stoop so low as to borrow a *camera*. The Canon AT-1 with manual exposure and nifty fifty lens was Sam's camera of choice, but the odds of his parents springing for one of those *on top of* tuition were too slim to calculate. On the other hand, he didn't see the harm in having a look at one, just in case.

He rode the Green Line into Boston to the cluster of camera shops on Bromfield Street where he'd gripped the Canon's body dozens of times before. At each shop, he gave the AT-1 an exhaustive inspection as if handling it for the first time. He attached and detached its lenses like a pro, adjusted its shutter speed selector dial, click by click, pressed firmly on its shutter release button, and knew precisely when to let go of the film advance lever just as it was about to snap back into place. The longer the Canon was in his hands, the more it seemed to belong to him; but the cost of a new kit was prohibitive, and used models were only marginally less expensive. And so the pleasure Sam derived from cradling his favorite camera wore off by the third or fourth recurrence of the afternoon.

Who was he kidding, anyway? There was no way his parents would pay for this camera—Jesus, his father's head would likely explode upon hearing the request. The only scenario Sam could envision in which he'd be bringing an AT-1 into class with him would be if he tightened his grip on the one currently in his hands and made a run for it.

Was that all there was to it? Was petty larceny the solution to all his problems? He weighed the pros and cons—leaning heavily toward the pros—before reminding himself that he'd been making steady pilgrimages to these very same shops for about five years now, was practically on a first-name basis with every employee up and down the street. The cops would be waiting to arrest him outside his apartment by the time he made it back.

On the subway home, tired and dejected, he caught himself as he was about to fall asleep on the shoulder of the woman seated next to him. She was old enough to be his grandmother, probably wouldn't have minded, but Sam felt embarrassed anyway. He exited the car one stop early, at Beaconsfield, cutting through backstreets and a playground to reach his apartment. Streaks of fading sunlight settled across rusted-out monkey bars and metal slides, and, everywhere he turned, leaves had begun to change color. Sam felt the keen absence of a camera.

He made it halfway through a M*A*S*H rerun and the cold spaghetti he'd been eating straight out of a can before passing out on his couch.

*   *   *   *

Davis phoned later that evening to invite him to a newly opened brewery in Kenmore Square. Davis and Perry, his best friends from high school, were sophomores at Boston College now and had access to an endless array of fake IDs. Phony out-of-state licenses were currently all the rage—the one they sold to Sam a few months earlier purported to be from Nebraska. Davis and Perry didn't play sports, belong to campus organizations, or pay much attention to their grade-point averages. Getting past the bouncers at trendy college bars was pretty much the focal point of their education.

"They make their own beer!" Davis said of this new place. "They've got flavors that'll blow your mind. Oatmeal, cranberry, pumpkin, blueberry, mint—believe it or not, they've even got chocolate!"

"How about peanut butter," Sam asked, still groggy from his nap, "do they have that too?"

"We'll be there after nine," Davis answered, not laughing, before hanging up the phone.

Sam approved of the bar straightaway. It featured massive, fully operational vats visible behind a plexiglass partition, oversized temperature gauges above each vat, and a system of copper, snake-like pipes overhead that, Sam assumed, either transported the beer from the vats directly to the kegs or were purely decorative.

Sam spotted Davis and Perry in a booth sipping identical foamy brown mixtures from pint-sized mugs. The three of them had known each other since the seventh grade, but in the past year or so Sam had begun to suspect that their friendship might have run its course: when they got together lately, Sam found it increasingly difficult to tell Davis and Perry apart. For the time being, however, Sam resolved not to examine their friendship too closely, for fear he might be left with no friends at all.

He ordered a blueberry beer from a passing waitress who seemed vaguely familiar. Out of nowhere, she yelled out: "Oh my God, you're Sam Jacobs, from Newton South! You were a junior when I was a senior!"

"Ah, the good old days," Sam replied.

"Weren't you in the school play in junior high?"

"Yeah, *Anything Goes*. I was the priest who got pushed off the boat in the first few minutes of the play. That was the beginning and end of my acting career."

"You had gray hair."

"It's funny you should remember that. It stained my jacket and hands."

The waitress's name was Meredith Comstock. She had dirty blond hair and tiny freckles across the bridge of her nose. Sam wasn't interested.

"Why the hell not?" Perry asked, once Meredith had departed.

"Because, for starters, we went to high school together."

"What kind of pathetic excuse is that?"

"What if we got into a serious relationship and decided to get married one day? Everyone would give us shit for having gone to high school together."

Perry shook his head in disgust.

After finishing his blueberry beer, Sam switched to pumpkin, his attention now focused exclusively on the hostess pacing back and forth near the entrance to the bar. Dressed in a tight black blouse and black miniskirt, she had short brown hair, a pale complexion, and clear blue eyes. She looked like a cross between Natalie Merchant and Audrey Hepburn, and Sam was instantly smitten.

"Guys," he announced to his friends, "I'm in love with the hostess."

"You always fall for the ones you can't get," Davis reacted, matter-of-factly.

"Yeah, but she looks like a cross between Natalie Merchant and Audrey Hepburn," Sam explained. Perry wasn't buying it, but that may have had something to do with his conviction that Audrey Hepburn had starred opposite Humphrey Bogart in *Casablanca*.

"Here I go," Sam declared, rising to his feet. "Notify my next of kin if I crash and burn."

He followed a trail of copper pipes to the front of the brewery, where the pretty hostess was now fiddling with bowls of matches and toothpicks.

"Is Meredith working tonight?" Sam asked her, his voice cracking.

"I saw her a minute ago," the hostess answered. "She's around here someplace."

"Okay, thanks," he said, nodding as he turned to make his way back to the booth. But his humiliation was too much to bear, and he spun around abruptly to face her.

"Believe it or not, I wasn't looking for Meredith," he confessed, words coming out fast. "I came up here to talk to you, but couldn't think of anything to say."

"Wait, your pick-up line is that you couldn't think of one? And I'm supposed to give you credit for that?"

"Clearly, I miscalculated."

"Self-deprecating humor masking feelings of inferiority," she said. "Strike two."

"Do you get approached a lot?"

"And what's *that* supposed to be, mock sincerity? Jeez, you really are terrible at this."

"Twenty years from now," he suggested, "you may miss the attention."

"Wow. Clear-cut signs of passive-aggressive tendencies. You're in therapy, right?"

"Do you like Vietnamese food?" he asked her.

"No!" she snapped.

"Me either," he said. "Can I have your phone number?"

"Are you kidding me?"

"How's this," Sam said. "I'll give you *my* phone number, and you can decide for yourself whether to call me or not."

"I have a better idea," she countered. "You march on back to your booth with your tail between your legs and forget any of this ever happened. Oh, and in case you're wondering, the bouncer's name is Bruce, and he's protective to a fault."

It never gets any easier, Sam lamented, averting eye contact with the pretty hostess and staring only at the matchbooks and toothpicks. "Bruce—got it," he muttered, his voice trailing off. "It's just that, I don't know, I was sitting over there, and I couldn't believe it. I mean, you look like a cross between Natalie Merchant and Audrey Hepburn."

"You don't know when to quit, do you?" she said, but laughing now.

Sensing he owed her something in the way of an apology, Sam managed a barely perceptible sigh before shuffling back to his table.

"Hey," she called out to him, "that last bit about Merchant and Hepburn—it wasn't terrible. You should've opened with that."

* * * *

By the time Sam's paperwork got approved, he'd already missed two weeks of Intermediate Photography. On his first morning of classes, he overslept. Rifling through the admissions packet the school had sent out, he was relieved to discover that he was only missing a darkroom block, scheduled each morning between nine and eleven. After darkroom, students took an hour break for lunch before regrouping for a lengthy afternoon critique session with the instructor. Sam had heard from a number of sources that these critiques could be brutal.

He didn't see much point in showing up to the darkroom on his first day of classes without negatives to print, so he crawled back into bed. Drifting in and out of consciousness, he gave serious consideration to skipping the afternoon block as well, given that he had no prints to present for review either. But even in his half-lucid state he seemed to grasp that if he followed this line of thinking to its logical conclusion, he'd miss the remainder of the semester; so he threw on some wrinkled clothes and arrived at the Museum School with a half hour to spare before critique.

As he stood outside the main building, alongside the school's gigantic rhinoceros sculpture, Sam's natural propensity toward self-doubt and second guessing returned with a vengeance. Why should he make his grand entrance at a new school when the other students in his class were still away at lunch? Vowing to return in time, he cut through the Museum of Fine Arts parking lot to the new I. M. Pei-designed West Wing, which had recently opened to wide acclaim. The enrollment packet Sam carried with him inside his knapsack contained paperwork for a student ID, and Sam assumed he could use that now to gain free admission to the museum's café, located inside. But the café's famously exorbitant prices gave him pause, so he changed direction yet again, landing at a nondescript sandwich shop on Huntington Avenue instead.

The place was empty, which seemed odd given the time of day and proximity to the school. Sam figured the students had good reason to avoid it, but he was running out of time and walked right up to the counter to order a hamburger.

His table faced a bulletin board that instantly grabbed his attention. "Take my cat, please—she's sweet and gentle," one message read, and, "Eight women needed for semi-professional 16mm. film" read another. Sam made quick work of his greasy burger while reading handwritten notices for guitar lessons, apartment subleases, and used furniture.

All at once, his heart sank. What the hell was he *doing* at this school, anyway? He wasn't even a formal student in any official capacity, so it stood to reason his classmates would never accept him as one of their own. And he'd already missed the first few weeks of the semester, putting him at even more of a disadvantage. He was certain to make enemies just by speaking his mind (this was a given), and, soon enough, his instructor would turn on him too (they always did). For Chrissakes, he didn't even own a camera! What was he *thinking*?

His parents had offered him one last chance to fix his life, and he'd already blown it. He'd made yet another catastrophic error in judgment. An interloper at a school where he didn't belong, he wanted nothing more than to get away as fast as he could.

That's when he spotted the message on the bulletin board that might as well have been written specifically for him. "Wanted: nice person to share driving on cross country trip to L.A.," the note read.

Sam dashed outside to the nearest payphone on Huntington to call the number. The woman who answered tried to explain that the note was many weeks old, and that the guy heading to California was already long gone.

Sam couldn't believe it. *That should've been me in that car*, he thought. *It should have been me!* And so he skipped the afternoon session after all and caught the next train to Brookline, where he returned to his bed exactly as he had a left it, sheets and blankets twisted up and hanging off the side.

1989

GOODBYE, CUTE BOY

It was at the start of last winter when I quit my job at the shoe store for no particular reason. I couldn't have picked a worse time to quit—I was three grand in the hole on my credit card, with less than a hundred bucks in my checking account—but it beat selling shoes. My parents phoned each night to confirm I'd eaten a nutritious dinner; I'd lie and tell them that I had, and they'd pretend to believe me. Each call from my parents adhered to the same recurring format, kicking off with deep concern for my general wellbeing and culminating in the series of steps I'd need to take in order to fix my life.

I became adept at recognizing the faintest hint of urgency that crept into my parents' voices as they guided each call to the same predetermined outcome. Boilerplate advice lurked around the corner of even our most innocuous exchanges, as if repeated exposure to the same worthless platitudes would allow them to sink in at last. You had to hand it to my parents: they were relentless. But even their most persuasive arguments faltered under the weight of constant repetition. Their proposed remedies grew so familiar as to take on the qualities of a mantra: apply to law school, find a girl, settle down. It was as if I suffered from a hundred diseases all sharing the same cure. Apply to law school, find a girl, settle down.

The lease on my Brookline Village apartment was about to expire, presenting me with one of those classic good news/bad news scenarios. On the plus side, I'd already paid my last month's rent, and could live rent-free for the next month until my lease ended. The bad news: I was about to step off a cliff. Desperate to avoid another job in retail, I informed my landlord that I'd be leaving by the end of November, a decision that came with immediate consequences: I'd have no choice but to move back into my parents' house in Newton Centre, where I hadn't lived since graduating college three years prior.

My upstairs childhood bedroom had by this time been converted into an office—stacks of paper three feet high were now positioned around it like various stages of an obstacle course—so I'd need to make do with the wood-paneled, musty storage room in their basement instead. My first week downstairs was devoted to a cascade of soap operas and talk shows; I'd sit in front of a junky, half-busted black-and-white TV for unknowable stretches of time, eating plain yogurt by the pint, straight out of the carton.

It seemed unlikely that I'd get around to solving any of life's great mysteries in my parents' basement, which suited me just fine: I had more pressing concerns on my mind anyway. Over breakfast one morning, I announced to my parents that I'd done a lot of thinking lately and had finally arrived at the decision to take the LSAT—the Law School Admission Test. This was, of course, the exact prescription my mother and father had been squawking about for years, so I made sure to credit their accumulated wisdom for my unexpected change of heart. "The next scheduled test date is in January, only five weeks away," I cautioned, "so I'll need to study a minimum of six hours per day, seven days a week. Honestly, I don't see how I can hold a job at the same time."

A switch had been flipped, and, in that very instant, everything changed between my parents and me. All at once, I'd miraculously transformed into the son they'd always wanted, and they were eager to make the most of it. Overflowing with unbridled joy, they lavished me with pocket money, began washing and folding my laundry, and more or less treated me like royalty. Their reaction, while predictable, was still troubling; I couldn't decide whether to feel grateful or more depressed than usual. (It was at about this time when I began toying with the notion that my parents in fact hated my guts.)

I picked up the necessary preparation books, sent in the application paperwork (at a cost of seventy-five dollars, which you-know-who were only too happy to cover), and got started on a five-week regimen of exhaustive study. Let me rephrase that: I endeavored to mentally prepare myself for the steep challenges that lay ahead of me. Wait, that's still not right. I need to be precise here—the LSAT is about nothing if not precision.

I lied my ass off.

I had no intention of ever applying to or, God forbid, *attending* law school. I just needed to hit the pause button on my life for a brief period as I sorted a few things out. Going through the motions of preparing for an entrance exam while living rent-free in my parents' basement was the closest I was likely to get to an actual plan.

Don't misunderstand me—I'm not a dishonest person by nature. I alternated between feelings of guilt about the fact that I was lying to my parents and the unwavering certainty that they surely deserved it. Either way, I didn't have any other cards left to play.

* * * *

The LSAT was divided into three sections: analytical reasoning, reading comprehension, and logic games.

Analytical reasoning, which was supposedly the least challenging section of the exam, was anything but. A typical question read: "There are ethical codes that all individuals require in order to exist, because all individuals require ethical codes in order to exist. Which of the following statements, if true, would undermine this argument? (A) All individuals require the same ethical codes in order to exist. (B) Not every individual requires the ethical code of integrity in order to exist. (C) Not all individuals must share the same ethical codes in order to exist. (D) Every individual requires the ethical code of honesty in order to exist. (E) No two individuals require any of the same ethical codes in order to exist." Trying to make sense of this was akin to getting bitten by one of those nightmarish Amazonian spiders that cause instant paralysis, except, in my case, the effects were restricted exclusively to my brain. It took enormous willpower on my part to maintain my concentration as I labored to narrow down my options. Whichever answer I eventually settled on seemed, at best, like a half-educated guess.

The next section, reading comprehension, consisted of rambling, drawn-out passages on such stimulating topics as photosynthesis or cellular mitochondria. These were subjects I couldn't get my head around in *school*, when I had *teachers* to explain them to me—what chance did I have of making sense of them now? Each time I reached the end of one of these long, excruciating paragraphs, I was more convinced than ever that I must be an undiagnosed dyslexic.

And lastly came the most infuriating section of all—logic games—sinister, convoluted riddles that proved all but impenetrable no matter how earnestly I aimed to solve them. "Three sets of identical twins, Amory and Amy, Garrison and Grace, and Martin and Margaret play at the beach. Amory, Garrison, and Martin are boys. Amy, Grace, and Margaret are girls. Each twin pretends to be one and only one of the following American Presidents: Washington, Jefferson, Lincoln, Roosevelt, Eisenhower, or Kennedy. More than one twin may pretend to be the same president, but if one twin pretends to be Washington, then his or her identical twin must pretend to be Lincoln. Amory and Margaret always pretend to be the same president. Garrison pretends to be Jefferson. None of the girls pretends to be Eisenhower. Neither Grace nor Martin pretends to be Kennedy. If Martin and Margaret pretend to be the same president, then which of the following is a complete and accurate list of the presidents Amory may pretend to be? (A) Washington, Kennedy; (B) Jefferson, Roosevelt; (C) Lincoln, Roosevelt; (D) Washington, Jefferson, Roosevelt; or (E) Jefferson, Lincoln, Eisenhower." I'd jot down all the various combinations, draw a makeshift diagram just as the preparation books had instructed, and, feeling wholly inadequate, stomp upstairs to the kitchen for a consolation bowl of mocha almond ice cream and another tub of yogurt.

One might conclude that I couldn't have cared less about my performance on this test, given that my motivation to take it in the first place was in service of an elaborate lie. But one would be wrong. I studied. That is to say, I studied for a minimum of two hours per day, or thereabouts. My reasoning was simple: it would have been impractical to bail on the exam entirely, as I knew my parents would insist on going over my score with a fine-tooth comb. Even so, my two measly hours of daily study kept getting whittled down, until, by the end of the second week, I was taking every other day off. I just didn't see the point in torturing myself. As far as I was concerned, only a masochist would study *harder* for a test he was certain to fail.

That's when things started to get a little weird. Out of the blue, I started feeling *happy*, happier than I'd felt in years. I was downright giddy on most days, sitting pretty in my basement hideaway, the door shut, my parents so detached from my daily life that they might as well have been out of the country. I could do anything I wanted down there, as long as it could be accomplished within the confines of my wood-paneled sanctuary. I listened to sports radio, read dirty magazines, and, before I knew what hit me, came up with a nifty idea for a screenplay.

I'd made several misguided attempts at screenwriting in years past, each time stalling out as soon as it became apparent there weren't enough hours in the day to complete a decent draft. But all of a sudden I had loads of time—more time than I knew what to do with—not to mention free room and board. I picked up an overpriced how-to book that purported to teach the three-act journey, or hero's structure, or something to that effect, and, armed with helpful pointers, was off to the races. (I kept an LSAT preparation book by my side at all times, should my parents decide to pay me any unexpected visits.)

Within days, I was astonished to discover that I was actually writing a screenplay! Scenes flowed effortlessly, one right after the other, as snappy dialogue burst from my imagination directly onto the page. I packed my script with romance, suspense, helicopters, explosions— all the good stuff—writing instinctively, in a dreamlike state of inspired dementia. The fact that I was working in utter secrecy, deceiving my parents with each new plot twist, only served to make the experience more thrilling.

I completed my very first full-length screenplay, "Dodging Bullets," two days ahead of the exam. I knew a guy from college who'd moved out to L.A. to work as an assistant at one of those big Hollywood talent agencies, so I called him up to gloat about what I'd just written. "It's worth a million bucks!" I promised, and he all but ordered me to overnight it to him that very afternoon. I printed it out on three-hole punched paper, found a couple of rusted brads lying around to bind it, and stuffed the whole thing into a giant manila envelope. My adrenaline now pumping, I sprinted through dirty snow to the Newton Centre post office, humming a song by Squeeze along the way. An overhead fluorescent tube inside the post office had gone out, and the whole place looked dark and gloomy; but I kept my sunglasses on nonetheless. I could barely see three feet in front of me, but I was overnighting a high-concept action thriller to an up-and-coming industry contact in Hollywood—how could I *not* wear sunglasses indoors?

On the eve of the LSAT, I felt some vague duty to prepare my parents for what would undoubtedly be a lousy test score. "I worked my butt off preparing for this," I asserted at the dinner table, trying my best to feign vulnerability. "It's the hardest thing I've ever done, I swear to God," I continued, laying it on thick. "Whatever happens tomorrow, you need to understand that I gave it my best shot, studying six, often eight hours a day, seven days a week. But there's something else you need to understand. This test was designed to weed out the smart kids from the rest of the pack. I never truly appreciated the significance of innate intelligence before I went through the process of studying for this exam. I'd always assumed that I could do anything I set my mind to, that I had the brains to accomplish anything. But after what I've experienced these past five weeks, I've come to realize that's not really the case. I studied as hard as I could, but at some point my practice scores stopped showing improvement, and I can now predict with a high degree of certainty what my eventual score will be. What I'm trying to explain is that, no matter how confident or relaxed I might feel tomorrow, it won't make any difference. It kills me to have to admit this, but there are brilliant people in this world, *geniuses*, who know how to come up with all the right answers—who are just plain *smarter* than me—and I'll never be one of those people, no matter how I try. I know you want me to make something of my life, and so do I; but I need to prepare you for the possibility, no, the *probability*, that I may not have what it takes to get into a top law school, or even a mediocre one, for that matter."

They hugged and kissed me, and wished me the best of luck, all the while imploring me not to feel anxious about my score. My father even insisted that I sit through half an hour of Mozart's Concerto for Flute and Harp—he'd read something in *The New York Times* about how listening to Mozart before a test made you smarter.

The next morning, I awoke at dawn, showered, ate a bowl of cereal, sharpened half a dozen number two pencils, and drove the few blocks to the Boston College law school campus, where the exam was being administered. There were at least twenty people waiting to take the test in the assigned classroom when I arrived, so I found an empty seat in the back, filled out some forms, and counted down the minutes before the LSAT was set to begin. And that was the exact moment when, once again, things got a little weird.

All of a sudden, I was overcome by a brand new sensation I'd never experienced before. Initially, I chalked it up to nerves, but soon enough I knew exactly what it was: goddammit, of all the corny, pathetic notions, I wanted to do well on this fucking test. I wanted to *ace* it. I wanted Harvard, Yale, Stanford. Nothing short of Ivy League would do. And I could do it, too! I could do anything I set my mind to! I had the brains to accomplish anything! Visions of Supreme Court clerkships and six-figure salaries danced inside my head as the proctor handed out the test packets and wished us all good luck. She might as well have been addressing *me* exclusively, wishing *me* good luck, because my life was about to turn around. I was only twenty-five—not exactly young anymore, but, come on, by no means ancient—and wasn't addicted to gambling or alcohol, much less cocaine, heroin, or any of those other hardcore substances, and had just completed the first draft of a blockbuster screenplay guaranteed to sell for a million bucks! Maybe, just maybe, I told myself, the world's not such a shitty place after all.

In February, I broke out in pimples, more of my hair than usual clogged up the shower drain, my contact in L.A. stopped returning my phone calls, and, icing on the cake, I received my LSAT results in the mail: 147 out of a possible 180, not even a good enough score to get admitted into a *second-tier* law school. Each day, a new brochure would arrive in the mail from yet another low-ranked program located in some far-off state, the kind of bottom-feeding place only too willing to take your money. So much for easy street.

And then, just as it appeared my life couldn't get any worse, my parents dropped the hammer: my only reason for taking the exam, they'd concluded, was to avoid finding a new job and another place to live. What's more, they'd been suspicious of my intentions from the very start.

I emphatically denied their accusations, but to no avail. I was a freeloader, pure and simple, and they considered it their obligation as good, decent parents to cut the umbilical cord—*cut it, cut it!*—notifying me that I had one month to find a steady source of income and another place to live before they'd throw me out onto the street and never speak to me again. Or something to that effect.

* * * *

I could type over fifty words a minute, so landing a temp job that paid ten bucks an hour was never too far out of reach. Boston was top-heavy with temporary employment agencies; if you knew your way around a fax machine and Microsoft Word, agencies couldn't place you fast enough. Over a three-week period in March, I temped at a hospital, a brokerage house, an insurance agency, and, adding insult to injury, a law firm. It was always the same routine no matter where I ended up: I wore a tie, khakis, and loafers, arrived by 8:30 a.m., typed memos, answered phones, sent faxes, made Xerox copies, took a half-hour (unpaid) break for lunch, typed more memos, answered more phones, sent more faxes, dropped off the overnight mail, and made more copies—all in anticipation of five o'clock, the freedom hour. The exhaustion I'd inevitably feel by the end of another monotonous workday stemmed as much from self-loathing as anything else.

On the off-chance that I'd cross paths with an attractive secretary at one of these offices, I'd go out of my way to appear charming—though I'd be lying if I said that I ever got anyone's phone number as a result. Even the most superficial exchange would sooner or later come around to the girl wanting to know what the hell I was doing *temping* for a living, and, because I had no satisfactory answer, she'd invariably lose interest in me by the close of the business day.

On subways to and from work, I'd pass the time reading paperback best-sellers about genetically engineered dinosaurs, renegade nuclear submarine commanders, or corruptible lawyers; either that or I'd scan the sports pages someone had left behind on the train. For the most part, it didn't matter what I was reading, just as long as I could avoid eye contact with all the other passengers.

Nearing the deadline my parents had set for me evacuate their basement, I scoured the help wanted and real estate sections of the *Globe*, searching in vain for the least objectionable job I might qualify for and an apartment I could realistically afford. A full-time job seemed unlikely, but, in due course, I came across a promising listing for an apartment in Allston—not the most desirable location in the world, unless you're partial to drunks, drug addicts, degenerates, or college students. Upon inspection, it turned out to be even worse than I had imagined—a tiny basement studio, cramped and dimly lit—but I was running out of time and had little choice but to sign the lease.

The rent, five hundred and twenty-five dollars a month, or about seventy hours a month consigned to temp hell, was twenty-five dollars *more* than what I'd been paying at my previous apartment in Brookline Village (I'd already inquired about getting my old unit back, but, predictably, they'd jacked up the rent as soon as I'd moved out). Meager paychecks from an assortment of employment agencies would be just enough to keep me afloat. In April, I rented a van to transport my futon, beloved Klipsch speakers, and childhood dresser to Allston, even managing to install privacy shades and hang up a few posters by nightfall. *This isn't so bad,* I told myself. *Some people have it a lot worse.* But it was bad, all right. By any objective measure, my new place was inferior to any apartment I'd ever lived in, dorms included. The carpet was a murky shade of green, the ceilings couldn't have been more than seven feet high, and the bathroom sink and shower were encased in a layer of mold and grime so impenetrable that none of my furious scrubbing could make a difference. Whatever natural sunlight there might have been—and there wasn't much to begin with—was obscured by privacy shades at all times of the day and night in order to prevent the constant stream of passing pedestrians in front of the building from getting a peek inside.

I hardly slept during my first three nights in the apartment, which was located only one block from a busy—and noisy—Brighton Avenue. Each night around 2:00 a.m., as the bars would begin the grueling process of kicking out all the drunks, I'd curl up in my futon with my hands pressed against my ears, hoping to block out the raspy voices of bitter alcoholics shuffling past my window.

The nearest subway stop on Commonwealth Avenue was a fifteen minute walk from my apartment, but pretty soon I learned of a bus route downtown that had a stop only a few blocks from my building. To my great surprise, I found that I vastly preferred riding at street-level to the experience of traveling underground. For starters, bus fare was only half the price of a subway token, and I could usually find a seat on most mornings, whereas on the subway I'd more often than not have to stand all the way into the city. But the best part of all was that I was able to shave about twenty minutes from every mind-numbing subway ride to and from the Financial District or Government Center that I assumed would be a permanent fixture of my life.

A typical bus ride involved a series of tasks both trivial and decisive: leaving my apartment at precisely the right time each morning so as to arrive at my stop just as a bus was pulling up; making sure to have exact change so I wouldn't need to jam a wrinkled dollar bill into the fare machine; and trying to snag a window seat to avoid getting my knees bumped by new passengers as they boarded.

One evening, waiting near City Hall for my Allston bus, I spotted two girls standing a few yards away who couldn't have been older than nineteen or twenty. One of the girls, a pretty blonde in a formfitting purple blouse and pink chiffon skirt, seemed to have sprung miraculously from the pages of a fashion magazine. There was a bit more mystery to the other girl—dark hair, wire-rimmed glasses, black T-shirt, ripped denims —although neither girl could have been accused of having much mystery to her at all, unless my trying to deduce whether they'd be taking the same bus as mine qualified as mysterious.

My bus arrived and, sure enough, both girls got on. I sat diagonally across from them, one row back, and immediately began to eavesdrop on their conversation.

"I only want the kind of glasses that block UV rays."

"I can't remember what I did with my lighter and it's bumming me out."

"Don't let me eat garlic again."

It was the most sustained interaction I'd had, albeit indirectly, with pretty girls in quite some time, and it was having an intoxicating effect on me. I invented lives for them around their truncated sentences: they were roommates, in all likelihood college students, already accustomed to preferential treatment by society in general and men in particular. They were admired, revered, coveted—yet all the while kept at arm's length from the general population, as if they were members of some endangered species. For my part, I viewed myself as little more than a tourist, gawking at them at the zoo.

A mile or so into the ride, I began to feel intensely self-conscious about all attention I'd been paying to them. That was about the time when a man in a pinstriped double-breasted suit boarded the bus. The girls spotted him straightaway, picking him out so fast, in fact, that it was reasonable to assume he was sending out a specific type of pheromone only other beautiful people could detect. They must have instantly recognized him as a member of their species.

The man was tall, in his mid-thirties, with meticulously groomed hair and sharply defined features. He was by far the best-looking man on the bus—I couldn't help thinking he must have been a lawyer—and in no time flat he emerged as the focus of intense scrutiny from the two girls.

"Hello, cute boy," the brunette said, loudly enough for the man to hear.

"Hello, cute boy," the blonde echoed.

"That's the type of guy I could go for," Brunette said.

"Hunkorama," Blonde said.

The man in the pinstriped suit was now grinning as he openly stared back at the girls.

Brunette: "He's a pretty boy. I like that."

Blonde: "Pretty boys are the best."

Brunette: "Married, you think?"

Blonde: "Who cares. Let him drop some cash on me. I can keep a secret."

Brunette: "You couldn't keep a secret if someone stapled your lips together."

The man heard every word of this, and, rather than ignore the girls, he winked at them instead. The girls' reaction was instantaneous and pronounced: they could hardly contain their excitement.

Brunette: "Saturday. My place. Drinks."

Blonde: "Then straight over to my place for dessert."

As the bus pulled into its next stop, the man got up unexpectedly and made his way to the exit doors, waving to the girls almost as an afterthought.

Blonde: "Oh no, he's *leaving*."

Brunette: "Wait..."

Blonde: "Goodbye, cute boy."

Brunette: "*Goodbye*, cute boy."

My own stop was still a few blocks away, but it couldn't arrive fast enough—I was in the throes of a full-blown panic attack. Over the course of the ride, I'd been waiting for the girls to turn around and speak to *me*, maybe invite me out for frozen yogurt or a cappuccino. But my common pheromones went undetected.

Unfortunately, I was seated behind the girls, so it was impossible for me to slip away undetected. My only way out was to walk right past them. But now, for reasons I couldn't quite explain, I *needed* the girls to take at least one cursory glance in my direction. Eye contact seemed out of the question—my eyes were fixed to the floor below me, and I was trembling—but I had to do *something*. And so, wavering toward the exit, I muttered under my breath: "You two are pretty funny, you know that?"

The words had spilled out involuntarily, as if they'd been spoken by someone else, and I knew right away that I'd made a terrible mistake. To avoid further degradation, all I could hope for now was for the bus to come to a stop as quickly as possible so I could get the hell out.

"Get lost, creep," either the blonde or the brunette called out in my direction as I pushed open the doors to make my escape.

1993

LITTLE DID HE KNOW

Primary accomplishments of my first twenty-six years: almost got killed in the third grade while riding my bike; lived in Paris for a brief time as a teenager; graduated college with a degree in English that turned out to be practically worthless; dropped acid once in Los Angeles; never held a job longer than three months; lost in tennis more often than I've won; masturbated a lot; seen way too many movies to count.

That just about covers it.

I probably ought to have more vices by my age. And I'm not just referring to the really bad things that could get me killed. I'm not even addicted to *coffee*, nor can I stand those craft beers everyone's constantly raving about. As for the other stuff, I'm way too much of a coward to experiment with cocaine or heroin. Let's face it: I'm a lightweight. Whenever I get together with friends to share a joint, I'm usually the first to pass out (though I seem to be handling this one pretty well). Like

I said, I dropped acid that one time in L.A. with a girl named Mackenzie, but I don't plan on repeating that experience any time soon. Mackenzie and I were at a party in Brentwood where some random dude was handing out free tabs, and within half an hour I was spinning around in circles on a shag carpet in the middle of a crowded living room. Mackenzie told me afterwards that my head nearly got stepped on a dozen times before she realized what was happening and swooped in to rescue me. Anyway, no more acid after that.

Idea for a movie: in the near future, the government encourages people to get stoned because it's no longer feasible to care for or control the exploding population anymore. It's kind of a "Brave New World" meets "The Futurological Congress" kind of thing, but with a modern twist. The masses are given unlimited access to free drugs, become addicted, and spend the rest of their days watching music videos (computer games are popular too, possibly more so—each game accompanied by an ear-splitting soundtrack). Beyond that, there's nothing much else to watch on TV. No movies, nothing with dialogue or character development or anything like that. Words are pretty much obsolete too, so books have ceased to matter. Most of these music videos don't even have to make sense, as continuity and logic are no longer considered necessary. All that it takes for a video to become hugely popular is a track with a memorable hook and a bunch of hypnotic visuals strung together in no particular order.

Should I try to cram this exposition into the first ten minutes of the movie, or use one of those *Star Wars* crawls instead to spell out the whole plot during the opening credits? Also, it feels as if this premise is lacking in many of the required ingredients of a typical Hollywood blockbuster. Like, where's the conflict? Okay, okay. The people being given these drugs are basically prisoners in walled-off cities. They roam around all day with their virtual reality headsets on, watching music videos every minute of the day. Most of the addicts have surgically attached waste-bags so they don't even need to interrupt their viewing in order to use the bathroom. And they're forced to eat their meals inside massive, prison-camp-style cafeterias, sitting at absurdly long tables to ingest bland, drug-laced slop. Oh, I know, there could be another drug secretly injected into their *food*, a chemical that's making everyone infertile. That way, when a person's body inevitably shuts down from all the drugs in their system, no one's leaving any babies behind.

Seriously? That's *still* not a story. Haven't I learned my lesson by now? Each commercially viable screenplay has to contain a series of seemingly insurmountable obstacles introduced in ascending order of difficulty within a three-act structure! I mean, *come on!* Okay, Jesus, hold your fucking horses, I'm getting to it. Outwardly, the addicts appear to be happy, or at least they *think* they're happy. They can't get enough of the free drugs and trippy music videos. But it turns out the government's ultimate goal is to completely and utterly control the masses. Oh my God, are you kidding me with this crap? We *know* this! Get on with the fucking movie already!

The rich receive all the spoils: lavish lifestyles, perfect health, gorgeous homes. They pay lip service to how awful the drugs are, how the government should do more to combat the problem, blah blah blah, when in fact the rich *benefit* from everyone else being addicted. Thanks to the drugs, rich people now have a limitless supply of resources, as the masses have been effectively neutralized.

Goddammit Ethan, that's *still* not enough conflict! Not to mention, it feels a bit preachy. No one wants to sit through a story with a political agenda. Jesus, I'm hungry.

Okay, I feel like I may have identified what's missing from this story. Drum roll...here it is. A *hero*. That's right, a fucking hero! He lives among the masses, but somehow he's able to break free from his addiction and think for himself for short periods of time, maybe by learning how to go with the flow and not waste his energy fighting against the effects of the drugs. He has figured out how to reconnect with reality without living in perpetual fear of his own emotions. But he's definitely *not* an artist—no fucking way! If anything, it's the artists who are the sell-outs keeping the entire repulsive system running smoothly.

Anyway, where was I? The hero—he could be a teenager, a Luke Skywalker type—manages to escape his walled-off city, hiding out among the rich. Pretty soon, he uncovers an even *bigger* plot by the *super* rich to get all the second-tier rich people addicted to the exact same drugs the masses are hooked on. The super rich want it *all* for themselves; they want *everyone* else either dead or incapacitated, so that maybe 100,000 people control the *entire planet!* The second-tier rich are oblivious to what's truly going on; as far as they're concerned, their existence is safe, natural, and drug-free. But *their* food is *also* tainted, so not only are they getting high without knowing it, but they're having fewer babies as well.

These second-tier rich folks get addicted in a comedic sort of way. They still wear expensive clothing, have cool jobs, etc., but they're watching music videos on the sly while slipping on their own virtual reality headsets every chance they get. Each day, more and more of these second-tier rich types are turning into junkies with gizmos on their heads, but all the while they remain in denial about their predicament. They don't have a clue what's really happening to them until it's too late and they've been sent off to live with the other junkies in the walled-off cities.

Second-tier rich people don't *know* what's happening to them, don't know their food is tainted. They pride themselves on being drug-free and pure, working out at the gym regularly to feel young and healthy. Their only concern, since they have gobs of cash, is to stay clean. But, see, the hero, this teenager, he's already familiar with how the drugs make you feel when you're high, so he *knows* there's something in the food second-tier rich people are eating. By the end of the movie, the hero exposes the entire diabolical conspiracy, except no one believes him. The second-tier rich are too satisfied with their own way of life to do anything to jeopardize the system, and instead make a conscious decision to ignore the hero's warnings. They'd rather delude themselves into thinking the system is fair and compassionate, simply because it's been fair and compassionate to *them*. It's literally killing them *too*, only more slowly.

That's kind of a downbeat ending, if I'm being honest. The hero fails in his attempt to save humanity, while the super rich get to hang onto all their wealth and power. I might need to figure out a way to toss in some kind of silver lining at the end.

I could totally write this, send out query letters, land an agent in L.A., and sell it to a movie studio for a million bucks. I'll follow the advice spelled out in all those screenwriting books I keep buying: assign individual scenes to index cards, split the story into three acts, and send my hero on a perilous journey during which the *external* obstacles he faces are intrinsically linked to the *internal* flaws he must learn to overcome—leading to lasting, positive changes in both his external and internal worlds by the end of the movie.

On second thought, I probably shouldn't get too excited just yet. I could really use another bowl of mocha almond ice cream right now, and maybe a quick nap. I'll revisit the whole idea in the morning, see if it still holds up.

* * * *

Uniformed landscapers pull wilted tulips out of the ground as I cross the Public Garden on the first morning of a new assignment. Ignoring swan boats and bronze ducklings, I set my sights on a row of bicentennial-era buildings in the distance, blocks from the gold-domed Massachusetts State House.

Boston Property Resources, a cooperative real estate investment trust company, is located on the top floor of a five-story, nondescript, red brick structure more or less indistinguishable from its neighbors. I have no idea what a cooperative real estate investment trust company is, nor do I intend to stick around long enough to find out.

I'm a temp, and, at the risk of sounding overly pretentious or ironic, temping has turned into one of the last remaining constants in my life. Locations vary, responsibilities fluctuate, but, to quote Led Zeppelin, the song remains the same. I answer phones, sort mail, and send faxes, all the while resigned to the crushing sameness of my routine, the nonstop shuffling from one set of mindless tasks to the next.

It turns out that Boston Property Resources is a small investment firm, its main windows overlooking the Common. The company has only three full-time employees: Hank Wincott, the vice-president and treasurer; Linden Rhodes, the president, whom I'll be reporting to directly (he's out meeting with prospective clients when I first arrive); and Shirley, the administrative assistant, the person I'll be filling in for.

Hank is likely in his forties, but comes across as much older. His most prominent feature is a shiny, bald head, shaped like an egg, with a face that's altogether colorless, as if he's not getting enough oxygen to his brain. The tour he offers me of the premises lasts about five seconds: it's just two private offices separated by a cramped, windowless corridor that was presumably intended as a passageway between the rooms but now functions as a makeshift outer office instead. This claustrophobic strip, accommodating a computer tower, telephone, and laser printer sitting atop an ancient wooden desk, is where Hank tells me to make myself "comfortable." He even has a name for this unfortunate space: "Shirley's workstation." With the tour completed, Hank scurries back to his office and slams his door, giving me no indication as to when he'll resurface.

Left to my own devices, I read a chapter from the latest Michael Crichton paperback, then another chapter, and another one after that. At lunchtime, I raise my voice to communicate to Hank—or, more accurately, to his door—that I'll be stepping away to get something to eat. No response. At least two more hours pass before he finally lets me know me what my responsibilities at this strange assignment will be.

"Boston Prop," as he refers to the company, enlists insurance companies and pension fund managers to, in his words, "syphon off" their real estate holdings into something called a "REIT," a real estate investment trust. Some of what Hank says gets through to me, the rest I block out entirely. If I had to boil it down to a sentence, I'd describe it this way: Boston Prop takes someone else's commercial real estate assets and converts them into REITs, essentially privately-traded shares of stock that can be bought and sold by institutional investors. But even as my body language communicates profound indifference, Hank seems intent on plowing ahead with his summary. The REITs, as far as I can tell, are in fact collections of properties, bundled together into something called a *tranche* (rhymes with staunch). Hank goes on to explain that Boston Prop arranges to lease these tranches to outside management companies, who are then responsible for finding tenants and overseeing the properties. The whole arrangement sounds a bit sketchy to me, if I'm being honest. What at first blush resembles a simple real estate transaction involving rented office space gets twisted around somehow to allow large pools of private investors to receive quarterly dividends based on the projected value of properties they don't really own or even manage.

At every step of the way, Hank boasts, Boston Prop charges a fee. They earn a commission when the properties are bundled, again when the REITs are sold to investors as stock, and yet again when outside vendors are contracted to manage the properties. That's the entire business model, or at least the gist of it, and it's not especially hard to grasp. Nonetheless, Hank keeps talking and talking, trying to impress upon me how necessary it is for me to "get it."

"What you must understand is that we've created a business model that essentially runs itself," Hank assures me, rubbing a food stain from his tie. "We've got every angle covered. We take a cut from the seller, a cut from the buyer, and a cut from all the players in between. And the best part is, we don't get our hands dirty and we *never* get burned."

After a single day at Shirley's workstation, deciphering page after page of handwritten notes that seem to go on forever, I'm about ready to kill myself.

"If a Cooperative REIT reaches the minimum value of required properties pursuant to the Agreement to Option Properties before the financial auditor/advisor for Boston Property Resources has completed its Property Exchange Protocol and Stock Valuation Protocol for the Cooperative REIT, the financial auditor/advisor will delay its mandate to execute the protocols of a subsequent Cooperative REIT reaching minimum value of properties until the Property Exchange Protocol and Stock Valuation Protocol of the previous Cooperative REIT has been completed and such Cooperative REIT has been closed..."

I'm no expert on the Geneva Conventions, but I wouldn't be surprised if inputting this nonsensical gibberish into a computer for hours at a time is just the sort of thing that might qualify as a war crime.

Linden Rhodes, the founder and president, rolls into the office just ahead of five o'clock.

"You must be the temp," he says, towering over my desk. The grip of his handshake is firm enough to break several bones in my startled fingers.

"I am."

"Frightfully bored yet?"

I shrug.

Mr. Rhodes is tall and wide, with fat, powerful features. His eyebrows and ears are especially fat, and his remaining hair—white like an albino's—seems to curl and twist in defiance of gravity. It's no easy matter trying to determine his age: his complexion, smooth and ruddy in parts, wrinkled and chalky in others, offers no clue.

"I own this company," he says in a low, gravelly voice that seems to dip in and out of a British accent. "On paper, that would make me the chairman, but I find it more expedient to introduce myself as president. I'm Linden Rhodes."

"Ethan Gill."

"That's a fine name, Gill. Easy on the tongue."

"It used to be Gilman, until my father changed it," I elaborate.

Mr. Rhodes squints dramatically, as if I've offended him somehow. "What's Hank got you working on?" he asks, changing the subject.

"I think it's something called an offering circular."

"You *think?*" Mr. Rhodes snaps at me, incredulous. "You don't *know* what an offering circular is?"

"Can't say that I do."

"And people wonder why this country is going down the tubes." He places a hand on my shoulder. "An offering circular happens to be the lynchpin of our entire capitalist experiment. It's how men with ideas approach other men, men with money. It's the nucleus of every worthwhile business plan. So tell me, how does it read? Have we got commas in all the right places?"

"It's a page-turner," I assure him.

He laughs. "Any messages?"

"On your desk."

He strides into his office, and I take one last crack at the contract I've been slogging my way through for the better part of the afternoon. But it's no use: there's at least a ten-second delay between my fingers and my brain. "The manfate of Boston Property Resources will be to leberage its balance sheeg," is the best I can manage under the circumstances, typos proliferating with alarming frequency, "by the issue of long terk, high credit-rated, level-pay bonxs, rated by Standard and Poots Corporation and Moofy's Incestors Services, Inc., and to use the profeeds of such issues to acquite additionak properties and to probide the golders of the Class A Vommon Stock with reboupment of a portion of their inbestment..."

At precisely five o'clock, Hank puts on his overcoat and makes a run for it; seconds later, Mr. Rhodes appears once more at my desk, this time holding a bottle of Scotch and two glasses.

"Care to join me?" he asks.

"No thank you. My stomach can't handle the hard stuff."

"Smart stomach."

He pours himself a double, takes a swallow.

"I prefer to end each workday with a belt of the good stuff. Otherwise, what's the point?"

Not the most airtight logic, I want to say.

"Inputting investment contracts all day can't be the most rousing of activities," he offers.

"It's fine. I mean, it's a little dry."

"Perfectly understandable. Not everyone can be expected to have an aptitude for high finance. I'm assuming you must have skills in other areas?"

"Oh sure. I currently specialize in failure and regret," I deadpan, and he almost does a spit take. I'll say this about Mr. Rhodes: he seems to get my jokes.

"No shame in that, Ethan. I've been involved in any number of foolish ventures in my day, I can assure you of that."

"Goes double for me," I answer, full of zingers all of a sudden.

"How long do you plan on staying with us?" he asks, shifting gears.

"Actually, I wanted to talk to you about that. Hank mentioned something about your assistant being away on maternity leave?"

"Indeed. Shirley had her fourth child over the weekend. She's a bona fide baby machine, that woman. I suspect she'll be out of the office another three to four months. Care to stick around until her return?"

"I hadn't given it much thought," I manage to respond, lying through my teeth.

"What we do here must seem dreadfully tedious from your perspective," he says, as if reading my mind. "But there's more to it than the inputting of a never-ending series of contracts. If you pay close enough attention, you might learn a thing or two. Of course, whether you decide to stay on or not is entirely up to you."

"I guess I could give it a try," I hear myself saying.

"Wonderful! I'm pleased. It will be good having you around, Ethan. Fresh blood, that sort of thing." He takes another healthy swig of Scotch. "You know..."

He drones on about market capitalization and risk capital methodology, my eyelids growing heavier with each new pronouncement. A job isn't worth doing unless it's done right, he expounds, replenishing his glass; it's only through achievement that a man can fulfill the promise of dignity, pride, and self-worth. Mind you, the creation of wealth out of existing wealth is not some cheap parlor trick or shady ploy. No sir, not by a long shot. The discipline of investment finance may seem inconsequential to a layman such as yourself, but it forms the basis of the most far-reaching economic system the world has ever known...

* * * *

The work isn't as awful as I originally feared, and my mood improves, albeit slightly, after a few days at Boston Prop. Hank and Mr. Rhodes remain embedded in their respective offices much of the time, on their phones. Unsupervised, I'm in no rush to input contracts, update spreadsheets, or keep track of schedules. Hank wasn't kidding when he said the business runs itself; for reasons I can't begin to comprehend, private and institutional investors across the country are snapping up shares of Boston Prop's REITs.

I'm a skeptical person by nature, but I'm beginning to come around to the notion that Mr. Rhodes may have cracked the code. Let's put it this way: if there's a secret to generating revenue out of thin air, Mr. Rhodes seems to have unlocked it. It's not enough to describe him as operating under a different set of rules—it feels as if he's playing a different *game*. Let the rabble thumb their noses at high finance while slaving away at their thankless, dead-end jobs, Mr. Rhodes is fond of saying. Let them blow wads of cash on lottery tickets while daydreaming of fortunes that will never materialize. Gambling is for suckers.

Now, to be clear, I don't subscribe to any of this. From my perspective, the single-minded pursuit of financial gain for its own sake is tragically misguided. After all, what could be more pointless and unsatisfying than a lifetime spent calculating projected quarterly earnings and adhering to a strict bottom line?

On the other hand, the dollar amounts involved in some of these transactions are staggering, and it's hard not to feel a certain amount of admiration for Hank and Mr. Rhodes's method of "siphoning off" commercial properties. The assignment itself continues to eat away at my soul, to be sure; yet I can't help but marvel at the way these two men approach their work with such unabashed pride.

Mr. Rhodes never wears the same Brooks Brothers three-piece suit on successive days. He smokes a type of Dunhill cigarette only sold at high-end tobacco shops, drinks premium, single-malt Scotch, and dines at the Ritz-Carlton whenever the mood strikes him (it's among my responsibilities to confirm his lunch and dinner reservations). Returning from a stroll one afternoon, he brandishes a seventeen-hundred dollar leather attaché case purchased on a whim, the price tag still attached. His Rolex is solid gold, his shirts crisply starched, the portable telephone he carries with him to his meetings the latest in cutting-edge cellular technology. The grin on his face says it all: I'm rich, and, if you have a problem with that, you can go fuck yourself.

I gather from snippets of conversation that Mr. Rhodes is married to a woman several decades his junior. Their primary residence is a townhouse on Beacon Hill, only a stone's throw away, but other properties include a beachside summer estate in Rockport and a "whenever-I-damn-well-please" two bedroom co-op on New York's Upper East Side.

My office duties continue to expand: pretty soon, I'm cutting checks from Boston Prop's corporate account for expenditures that, on their face, strike me as conspicuously personal. Mr. Rhodes belongs to a half dozen of the most exclusive clubs in Boston as well as Manhattan, his dues paid through Boston Prop's corporate account. A six-month membership at a private

New York City club costs upwards of nine thousand dollars—an easier pill to swallow, I imagine, when his company is footing the bill. The maintenance fees and basic utilities on his Beacon Hill townhouse are paid by Boston Prop as well, as are varied disbursements to building managers, doormen, and caretakers at each of his properties. The company pays for all of it, though I doubt these expenses would slip past even a cursory examination by the most forgiving auditor at the IRS.

The irregularities go beyond a cascade of membership fees and monthly charges. Instead of using a credit card to make high-end purchases, like any normal person would do, Mr. Rhodes maintains store credit at establishments up and down Newbury Street— receiving mailed invoices from the stores themselves, as if it's the 1920s or something—each statement paid directly by Boston Property Resources.

I'm cutting checks for thousands of dollars from the company account to Brooks Brothers, for example. His black, navy, and gray pinstripes of choice run nearly two grand apiece. How many wool suits does one middle-aged, overweight man need? And that's not even taking into account his weekly dry-cleaning bills, which are astronomical, and also expensed to the company. As I close out my first month at Boston Prop, Winston Flowers sends over a bill for *twenty-six hundred dollars*; that one too, along with every other questionable invoice that lands on my desk, gets paid by company check, although I've yet to see a single bouquet around our drab, colorless office.

I'm fairly certain Mr. Rhodes is treating Boston Prop as his own personal piggy bank. Under normal circumstances, this would be a red flag. But these are not normal circumstances. Here's the thing: no matter how much money he withdraws from the corporate account, a seemingly endless rush of new funding arrives each week to replenish the balance sheet. My heart races as I record my first fifty thousand dollar wire transfer, an extraordinary occurrence that is followed in quick succession by another transfer of seventy-five thousand, and then, astonishingly, by yet another for a *hundred thousand dollars!* The whole goddamned financial world might as well be investing in Boston Prop's REITs, and there's no conceivable way Mr. Rhodes could spend all the money fast enough.

Like clockwork each evening, once Hank has made another of his hurried escapes, Mr. Rhodes saunters over to my desk holding his customary glass of Scotch.

"Congratulate me. We closed a deal for Automated Tech's pension fund," he reports tonight.

"Hey, that's terrific," I answer, feigning interest.

"Their commercial holdings are valued in excess of one hundred million dollars, Ethan. You *do* know what we charge in fees and commissions, don't you? Even a slacker like yourself can appreciate that many zeroes."

I do a few quick calculations in my head (Boston Prop charges half a point per converted property). "*Five million?*" I say, not at all sure if my math is correct.

"Perhaps from now on you'll pay more attention," he laughs. "It never occurred to me when I dreamed up this nifty little scheme that it would succeed to such an astonishing degree. In the back of my mind, I assumed companies would have to be *mad* to hand their real estate assets over to us."

"Why do you think they do it?"

"I've got the magic touch, my boy. I can turn a portfolio of drab commercial properties into gold."

"I've never been around this much money before," I confess.

"Few have. There's a trick to it, you know. Treat each million as if it were the equivalent of pocket change and you're well on your way to gaining command over your finances."

"Aren't you oversimplifying that a bit?"

"How so?"

"Don't you need the million first?"

"No, my boy—not true, not true at all. All that's required is for you to convince others that you can get your *hands* on it."

Mr. Rhodes downs his drink before clearing his throat. "What would you say to earning a bit of extra income on the side?" he asks, seemingly out of the blue.

"It would depend on the circumstances, I guess."

"I have a dog, a Brittany Spaniel. His name is Sebastian. He's a purebred pointer, a fully trained hunting animal. Make no mistake, he's a stone cold killer. He can be downright lethal. I've personally witnessed him tear the guts out of a feral cat while it was still breathing."

"How do I fit in?" I say, squirming in my seat.

"The thing of it is, I can't seem to find the right fellow to walk him. It's less of an issue on the weekends, when Sebastian's able to tire himself out darting up and down the shore or roaming the woods behind the house, hunting critters. But we don't get up to Rockport nearly as often as we'd like."

"Are you looking for someone to walk your dog, Mr. Rhodes?" I interject, catching on.

"Sebastian sits around the apartment all day, getting fat and lazy. Edward, the daytime doorman in our building, used to take him on his afternoon walks, but that's no longer an option. Some weeks ago, a resident in our building acquired a poodle, and the first time Sebastian crossed paths with that little rodent of an animal in our lobby, he nearly bit the poodle's head clean off. Edward had no choice but to kick Sebastian as hard as he could—another second or two and my dog would have snapped that puny creature's neck—but the kick sent Sebastian flying clear across the lobby! To this day, he holds a terrible grudge. He *loathes* Edward. Ever since, I've been through one dog walker after the next, but no one seems up to the task. I'll pay you twenty-five dollars a day, five days a week, to accompany Sebastian to the Esplanade—and that's on top of what you'd already be earning during that same hour from your agency."

"Hang on—you wouldn't deduct the time from my timesheet?"

"Precisely. Are you even aware what your agency charges us for your services?"

"I asked once, but they wouldn't tell me."

"Eighteen dollars an hour," Mr. Rhodes blurts out with obvious satisfaction. "Of that amount, I presume you only see ten?"

I nod.

"My God, Ethan. They're making an *eighty* percent commission off your work! It's downright extortionate, and I should know—I have experience in such matters."

"It's better for everyone if I don't think about it."

"That's where you're mistaken. You're being taken advantage of, young man. You *need* to think about it. Ten dollars an hour doesn't amount to very much, not after the federal government has taken its pound of flesh. How do you expect to amount to anything in this world on ten measly bucks an hour? I'm offering to supplement your income to the tune of five hundred dollars per month, *cash*—one hundred percent tax free, it goes without saying."

There's no doubt an extra five hundred dollars a month would go a long way toward paying down my ballooning credit card debt and digging me out of a rather sizable financial hole.

I shake hands with Mr. Rhodes, my grip noticeably firmer than usual.

* * * *

On a bright June day, I accompany Mr. Rhodes to his personal residence, breaking a sweat as I labor to keep pace. Again, I wonder about his age. Fifty? Sixty? Is he a grandfather?

The apartment is located in the heart of Beacon Hill, on a narrow, secluded cul-de-sac blocks from Charles Street in one direction and Mount Vernon Square in the other. His unit is on the top floor of a brick, three-story townhouse as old as Boston itself. We're met in the lobby by the infamous doorman, Edward the dog kicker, to whom I'm introduced as "Ethan Gill, a first-rate fellow." Edward, a somewhat decrepit old man with sunken cheeks, has presumably been expecting us and greets me with a spirited grin.

The building's elevator is one of those ancient, rickety models with a metal lattice gate that creaks open and slams shut. Mr. Rhodes and I ride it to the third floor, where we exit straight into his living room.

His apartment resembles the kind of place I'd expect to see from behind a velvet rope in a historic home that's been converted into a museum. There's little opportunity to appreciate the refined surroundings, however, as Sebastian, growling, comes crashing down the hallway towards us, his paws clicking loudly on the hardwood floors. He isn't a particularly large animal, but he's fast and spry, with ominous teeth on full display, and now I'm starting to question whether I'm going to make it out of here alive.

"He's suspicious of strangers," Mr. Rhodes cautions. "I'm afraid you'll need to let him register your scent."

"You mean *smell* me? Oh my God, you can't be serious." As I extend my hand for Sebastian to sniff, I'm convinced he's going to bite it off.

While it's true that Sebastian is, for the most part, utterly terrifying, it's hard to deny his charm. He's got floppy ears, a brown and white spotted coat, and a prominent black nose.

"He's a marvelous dog in most respects," Mr. Rhodes states, "with one or two minor deficiencies. He's a bit of a snob, I'm sorry to say."

"A snob? I don't understand. Is he into opera or something?"

"That's clever, Ethan, but not what I had in mind."

"I don't get it then. Is he a picky eater?"

"It's nothing to concern yourself with," Mr. Rhodes assures me, speaking more formally than usual, as if the apartment has brought out his inner aristocrat. "From time to time he's been known to exhibit a distaste for certain ethnic groups, that's all."

"Your dog's *racist*, Mr. Rhodes?"

"I wouldn't put it quite as crudely as that. At the risk of offending your delicate sensibilities, I'd describe him as somewhat disinclined toward darker-skinned individuals."

"Maybe you're just projecting," I suggest, and Mr. Rhodes lets out a hearty laugh.

"The jury's still out on his opinion of Jews," he bellows, slapping me on my back, still laughing. "Why don't I give you the nickel tour. He'll stop yapping in a minute or two."

We proceed down a long, dimly lit hallway to the kitchen, dining room, library, and outdoor terrace, each room somehow more perfect than the last. In the dining room, Mr. Rhodes points out a portrait of his grandmother, painted by none other than John Singer Sergeant; in the library, he reveals an extensive collection of first editions by Mark Twain and Henry James. Swinging open a set of French doors leading to the terrace, I'm greeted to a symphony of chirping birds and a more or less unobstructed view of sailboats on the Charles. Flanked on either side by swaying trees, red brick, and weathered cobblestone, it seems unlikely that I'll ever come across a more agreeable place on earth.

"That's the gist of it," Mr. Rhodes says. "There are three bedrooms facing east, nothing too elaborate."

"It's a terrific apartment."

"It's been in my family for generations, hasn't changed much over the years." He glances at his watch. "I'm needed back at the office. Will you be all right?"

"I sure hope so."

"Don't concern yourself with cleaning up afterwards," he advises me.

"Cleaning up...you mean Sebastian?"

"He's got an area marked out in the tall grass to conduct his business, away from the tourists. He's quite civilized when he wants to be, values his privacy. Just cross the footbridge to the Hatch Shell and follow the river north. Take your time, Ethan, and be sure to let him off his chain once you reach the Esplanade. He won't get far."

"Uh, hang on, should I be doing that?" I ask.

"Trust me, it's nothing to worry about. Sebastian has run away plenty of times and has always found his way home. He knows where his bread is buttered, that's for damn sure. Besides, there's little chance you'll manage to keep up with him while he's on his leash. He's a hunting dog, Ethan. He was bred to hunt—it's been genetically imprinted into his DNA. It would be the worst kind of cruelty to deny him his nature, don't you think? As soon as you reach the Esplanade, let him off the chain."

We circle back to the elevator on the far end of the living room.

"Come on now, Sebastian," Mr. Rhodes hollers, "Ethan's taking you out!"

Sebastian's barking intensifies as he jumps higher and higher into the air, his tail wagging excitedly. Mr. Rhodes attaches the leash while cooing into Sebastian's floppy ears: "Gonna kill a squirrel, aren't you boy?" and, "Yes, gonna decapitate it with your great big teeth." We ride the elevator down to the lobby, where Edward keeps his distance.

"Take all the time you need," Mr. Rhodes calls out, before disappearing out the front door without so much as a wave to Edward, Sebastian, or me.

"You'll exit from the back," Edward mutters, leading us past storage rooms and a modest kitchenette. Sebastian's thunderous bark continues to ring in my ears.

Outside, I make the mistake of loosening my grip ever so slightly on the leash, and Sebastian almost runs away without me. I'm immediately disabused of the notion that I'll be able to impose my will on this animal: as I grab the leash now with both hands, Sebastian and I tear down the street in an all-out sprint, but the leash doesn't seem to have any effect on his velocity. If anything, Sebastian picks *up* speed as we near the park. However fast I try to run to keep the chain from tugging at his neck, it's impossible to create any slack between us. On the footbridge above Storrow Drive, we shoot past joggers and rollerbladers as if they're standing still.

A cramp begins to form beneath my ribcage that requires immediate attention as my lungs cry out for more oxygen. By the time we reach the Hatch Shell, I'm doubled over in pain, my mouth wide open in a crude attempt to suck in as much air as I can.

I unhook the leash, and, in the time it takes me to refill my lungs, Sebastian has already crossed to the far side of the Esplanade. I'm in no condition to give chase, and start to panic about everything that could go wrong. If Sebastian were to decide to attack a newborn baby and swallow it whole, there wouldn't be a goddamned thing I could do to prevent it.

All of a sudden, Sebastian freezes dead in his tracks, his back and neck muscles stiffening as his eyes lock onto a chubby little squirrel foraging in a patch of overgrown grass. The squirrel is likely searching for a buried acorn, blissfully unaware of what's about to transpire. Sebastian moves so discreetly as to give the impression he's standing still—step, pause, step, pause—the distance between him and his target compressing incrementally.

Maintaining a rigid stance, Sebastian seems to float across the tall grass with what can only be described as a murderous glint in his eye. Before long, he's less than five yards away from his prey, his razor-sharp teeth poised to slam down hard on the squirrel's insignificant, furry frame. I consider throwing a pebble at the squirrel in order to spare its life, but decide it's not my place to interfere.

The stupid critter doesn't react until Sebastian is already airborne, and, finally aroused, it attempts a desperate escape toward the nearest elm tree. Halfway to the drooping elm, a new idea seems to take hold inside the squirrel's pea-sized brain: it'll be dead before it ever reaches that tree. Maybe it's not so stupid after all.

Veering off, the squirrel initiates a series of zigzagging maneuvers intended to wear out its attacker. All the while, Sebastian, undeterred by the added exertion, manages to shrink the distance between them. In the next instant, he makes his final, decisive push, biting down hard on the squirrel's fluttering tail.

The squirrel furiously attempts to squirm away as Sebastian keeps tugging and tugging on the end of its tail. Had Sebastian gotten hold of more tailbone and less fur, the resulting spectacle would no doubt have been gruesome. Instead, the tiny creature is able to slide its bushy tail right out from between Sebastian's protruding teeth.

I'm feeling strangely euphoric as I watch the luckiest creature on the planet bound up the trunk of an elm tree, out of harm's way. The squirrel climbs higher than it needs to, to the tallest branch, before determining it's safe to let its guard down. Perched a dozen feet above us, its tiny chest heaving in and out, the little squirrel glares down at Sebastian and me for a very long time, as if to say, "you sons of bitches, you goddamned sons of bitches."

* * * *

I'm not trying to insinuate myself into Mr. Rhodes's orbit—it was the furthest thing from my mind when I agreed to stay on longer than anticipated. But you never know where life will take you. As I settle in for a third month at Boston Prop, I continue to adapt to the vagaries of the assignment.

The company feels different in every conceivable way from all the other places I've ever worked at. "Unconventional" doesn't even begin to describe it. Each afternoon, rain or shine, I take Sebastian on another of our nerve-wracking adventures through the Esplanade, where he picks at scraps of bread and sandwich meat left behind by tourists while trying his best to murder squirrels. I'm spared from having to clean up after him, thank God: just as Mr. Rhodes promised, Sebastian can be counted on to crouch discreetly at the river's edge, whatever he leaves behind concealed by thick patches of wild reeds.

Our walks are perhaps the least unusual part of my job. I'm not even sure if I understand exactly what my job *is* anymore. I'm clearly a kind of personal assistant, but who is my employer—Boston Prop or Mr. Rhodes? I'm not even sure there's any discernible difference between the two entities anyway. Maybe the whole operation is just an elaborate front, a carefully constructed facade designed to obscure whatever the hell it is that Mr. Rhodes and Hank are *really* up to, hiding out each day in their respective offices.

It's never a good idea to speculate about such matters, but how else am I supposed to pass my free time? Call it a hunch or a gut feeling, but I just can't shake the notion that Mr. Rhodes is no expert in commercial real estate. He strikes me as one of those eccentric, old-money types, always on the lookout for novel ways to spend his inherited fortune. Perhaps, while lunching at one of the half-dozen private clubs he belongs to, he eavesdropped on a conversation about bundling commercial properties and selling them off as investable shares, and decided to have a go at it himself. I'm just spitballing, obviously—I could be way off base— but it's the only scenario that makes the slightest bit of sense to me. After paying a lawyer to set up his company, all Mr. Rhodes would've needed to do was pick up the phone and reach out to old prep school or university buddies who'd gone into careers as bankers or investment managers. Every other aspect of Mr. Rhodes's life seems to have come easily to him—why should Boston Prop be any different?

The first chance I get to meet his decades younger, absurdly gorgeous wife, Cynthia, she's inches away from me, leaning against my desk, dressed in a tight leather skirt, black pantyhose, and suede boots that reach all the way to her knees; my brain starts spinning so fast it's a wonder I don't pass out. She's twirling a finger through her flowing brown hair, joking with me about how I've been inside her apartment and, for all she knows, could have rifled through her underwear drawer.

I'm having an out-of-body experience—it reminds me of that time I took acid—but even in my impaired state I'm cognizant of the fact that Cynthia and I are having the sort of exchange temporary office assistants don't generally have with their bosses' wives. And neither is it standard practice to be notified a few hours afterwards that I won't be returning to Boston Prop the following morning because that same boss's wife has determined I'm to be *her* personal assistant instead.

Should I agree to any of this? Probably not. I think it's fair to say most temps in a similar situation to mine would no doubt have refused the opportunity. But were any of *them* positioned near enough to Cynthia to smell her perfume or catch a glimpse of her slip as she crossed and uncrossed her legs?

I think not.

And what about Mr. Rhodes? Shouldn't *he* have been the one to get across to his wife that I'm serving two pivotal functions at his company—office lackey and dog walker—and am therefore indispensable?

"Ethan," he groans at the five o'clock hour, his Scotch already poured, "I'm going to miss having you around."

* * * *

Nothing about the way I lurch from one job to the next seems routine, and yet none of it seems quite out of the ordinary either. Donna, my long-time representative at the employment agency, doesn't chew me out for bailing on a steady assignment, as I assumed she would. It turns out that the company where Cynthia works already had an arrangement with my agency, making for a relatively seamless transition. The abrupt switching from one assignment to the next that I experienced as jarring and strange is apparently business as usual to everyone else.

The next morning, I ride the subway a few extra stops into the city before grabbing a bagel and cream cheese at whichever coffee shop has the shortest line of customers. Determined not to arrive even one minute late, I wolf down my breakfast while power-walking to the steel and glass office building in the Financial District where I've been directed to appear. I'm still wiping cream cheese from my lips as I ride a crowded elevator up to the fifteenth floor and the expansive front lobby of Hendrick and Lambert Consulting, at precisely nine o'clock.

"I have an appointment with Cynthia Rhodes," I announce to the receptionist, who pauses a few seconds longer than I would have liked before directing me to have a seat. I'm about to skim through the latest issue of *Decadence* magazine on the coffee table in front of me when the receptionist conveys new instructions: "Down the hall to your left, third door on the right. She's expecting you."

I've spent the better part of my adult life in offices indistinguishable from this one. I pass Xerox machines, water coolers, flickering computer monitors, and row upon row of cubicles—all of it a welcome sight after the relative isolation of Boston Prop.

Cynthia Rhodes's office door is wide open when I arrive. I knock softly, and, next thing I know, her disembodied voice travels through an adjacent room before reaching me.

"Ethan, come in! Close the door behind you, and don't mind the mess."

Her office is divided into two sections. The area out front features computers, laser printers, beige metal bookshelves, and an enormous dark grey metal desk. It's a nondescript workspace without windows, and it's where I'm presumably to be situated. In order to enter Cynthia's larger, brighter, and more tastefully furnished private office, a person must pass through this outer room first.

Stacks of binders, brochures, folders, and pencils are strewn about the floor in her private office, but I hardly notice...Cynthia Rhodes is stunning. Her chestnut hair, streaked both light and dark, falls across her freckled, tanned shoulders. In place of yesterday's leather skirt, she's now dressed, somewhat to my astonishment, in a silk white blouse with spaghetti straps, a pair of ripped, formfitting blue jeans, and cowboy boots.

"I misplaced a damn file," she says, without looking up, "and now I can't find the fucking thing anywhere."

I'm having heart palpitations. "You want some help?"

"Let me decide if I'm gonna hire you first. Then you can crawl around on your hands and knees, if that's what it takes."

"Yeah, okay, sure," I manage to say, my legs buckling. A few seconds earlier, I was under the impression that I was already hired.

"Any trouble figuring out which building was ours?" she asks, standing straight now and finally making eye contact with me. "It can get a little confusing with all these damn cookie-cutter high-rises that keep popping up."

"Um, no. I've temped on this street half a dozen times before. Three companies on this very block, as a matter of fact."

She smiles. "Have a seat."

The only chair I can find is the one located behind her desk, but she gestures to another one in the corner of the room with stacks of folders on top of it—though it doesn't appear as if anyone's sat in it for months. "Just clear that crap off and drag it over, will ya?" she says, sinking into her fabric swivel chair.

"So, you must be asking," she starts, once I'm seated across from her, "why on earth would I suddenly poach the one and only Ethan Gill from right under my husband's nose? He's none too pleased with me, I can promise you that."

"I guess I am a little curious."

"You made quite an impression over there. Linden spoke so goddamned highly of you, it was starting to get on my nerves. Each day, it was Ethan this, Ethan that. And then you had to go and pass the hardest test of all."

"I wasn't aware of any test."

"You walked the fucking dog, Ethan, and lived to tell about it. After that, there was no way I was gonna let the old man have you all to himself."

"Sebastian's not so bad once you get used to him."

"I'm plenty used to him, and still can't stand the fucker."

I'm too nervous to laugh. I'm too nervous to do *anything.*

"Donna faxed over your résumé this morning," she continues. "It's not a train wreck or anything, as far as these things go, but it doesn't tell the whole story, now does it? I mean, it reads like a random list of unrelated assignments, and I can't for the life of me detect any rhyme or reason behind your choices. So I called Donna about half an hour ago, and she and I had a pretty lengthy discussion about you, just so I could get a fuller picture. Care to know what she said?"

"Uh, if you —"

"Don't freak out, it's nothing too embarrassing. She was mostly complimentary, you'll be happy to know. But she did mention a few things that caught my attention. I mean, I've never met this lady, you understand, and, completely unprompted, she shares with me that she feels protective of you—that you, and I'm quoting now, bring out her *maternal* instincts. Now what the fuck is *that* supposed to mean?"

"I have no idea."

"Not very fucking professional on her part, I'll tell you that."

"I honestly don't know why she said that," I state, sensing that I must be in trouble somehow.

"Yeah, well, it's highly inappropriate. So, do you want this job or not?"

"I don't even know what it is yet."

"You'd be working for me—what else do you need to know?"

She laughs at her own joke.

"Fair enough," I respond in earnest. "When do I start?"

"Easy there, hotshot. Did you think this interview was strictly a formality?"

"Wait, so I don't have the —"

"I'll ask the questions, if that's all right with you. It says here you attended UMass Amherst. Studied English, huh? What can you tell me about that."

"There's not much to tell."

"Did you like it?" she asks.

"Did I *like* college?"

"Personally, I couldn't wait to get the fuck out. What a huge fucking waste of time and money, if you want my honest opinion. So, yeah, I want to know if you liked it."

"Well, in that case," I begin, "I *did* sort of like it, but not for reasons that had anything to do with the courses, or the professors, or any of the friends I made there. And it wasn't because I was desperate to ditch my parents either. What I liked best about college was the free time. I had *loads* of free time. I never had to pay much attention to what I was studying, or to my grades, or to what I was supposed to be doing with the rest of my life. I'm pretty sure I was in a daze half the time. Friends would walk right past me, waving their arms to get my attention, and I wouldn't even notice. At some point I discovered that you could schedule all your classes on the same three weekdays and get two extra days off. Or you could stay in the library until midnight, wandering the stacks until some obscure book caught your eye. Or maybe just walk down to Amherst Center and find something interesting going on there, even if it was just walking through the old cemetery to hang out in front of Emily Dickinson's grave. I guess that's what I miss the most."

"Time."

"Yeah," I say, proud of myself, sensing that my response was more than adequate.

"I buy it," she says. "I miss my free time too. What should we cover next?"

"I could list all my favorite movies," I suggest.

She laughs again.

I breath easier, confident in my ability to ignore the unwelcome erection I've been contending with for the better part of five minutes by staring at the pastel-colored poster of a tropical island vista on the wall behind Cynthia. But inevitably my gaze returns to her silk white blouse and its plunging neckline.

"And now you've been out of school, what, five years?"

"Sounds about right," I say.

"And judging from this chaotic mess that you call a résumé, you've bounced around plenty, from one job to the next."

"That's one way of putting it."

"You gonna quit on me in two months, Ethan?"

The directness of her question catches me off guard. "Maybe four," I answer, confident now that the job interview portion of our conversation has ended, and that I'm now free to trade witty banter with the most beautiful woman I've ever laid eyes on.

"You gonna quit on me in *four* months, Ethan? Because free time is a luxury you won't have in this office. Your time will belong to *me*, you understand? I'll pay you more than my husband did—and I know all about his under-the-table dog-walking shenanigans, by the way—but you'll have to earn every penny of it. Unlike Linden, I don't operate at half speed, and if I hire you, you won't either. What exactly did Donna tell you about this place?"

"Motivational seminars for corporate executives, I think. I'm not entirely sure."

"We charge outrageous sums of money to teach managers how to be a little less putrid at their jobs. This department, *my* department, reports exclusively to the partners upstairs. I keep track of spending, quarterly budgets, and client retainers, but I'm in no way associated with the accounting department. I answer to the sixteenth floor and no one else. And when I describe it as *me* doing this, or *me* doing that, I'm not just blowing smoke up your ass. I *am* the department. You're looking at it. There was another chick who shared this office with me when I first came aboard, but she couldn't handle the stress so I had to send her packing lickety-split."

Cynthia leans forward, the neckline of her blouse revealing more cleavage than perhaps its designer intended. She continues, "I'm a wizard when it comes to math, but I can also be a bit of a handful. It's just how I'm wired. It might be a personality disorder of some kind. Whatever the reason, people around here tend to hate my guts."

"That can't be true," I object.

"Which reminds me of the other thing Donna said about you. That you were *adorable.*"

"She did not."

"She most certainly did."

"I wish she hadn't said that."

"Should I have a word with her about it, Ethan?"

I can't tell if she's being sarcastic or not, and anyway, my brain is still trying to catch up to what Cynthia said a few seconds back.

"How could anyone hate your guts?" I ask her.

"The partners upstairs tolerate me as long as I keep saving the company boatloads of cash. The consultants on *this* floor live in perpetual fear that I'll sniff out every rotten discrepancy they've tried to slip past me in their expense reports, and are smart enough to stay the fuck out of my way. As far as the rest of these clowns are concerned, I'd say half the women around here want to shove me out the nearest window, and half the men just want to get inside my pants. And if you work for me, mark my words, every stinking last one of these fuckers will hate you too. You still want the job?"

Now it's my turn to lean forward. I clench my teeth and stare into her steel blue eyes. "I'm your man," I promise.

* * * *

I mark time in my apartment waiting for the phone to ring, dreaming of Cynthia Rhodes. There's no point pretending I'm not already in love with her— or something to that effect. I get an erection every time I think about her, even if it's only in passing. That's not to imply I've gone completely over the deep end. A part of me still questions the wisdom of trading a low-stress gig at her husband's sleepy little company with a new assignment so fraught with obvious danger. I seesaw between wanting to follow Cynthia to the ends of the earth one minute to begging Donna at the temp agency to renegotiate my return to Boston Prop the next. As usual, I'm stuck somewhere in the middle, unwilling to make any decision whatsoever.

"Cynthia wants you," Donna notifies me at last, ringing me up after three excruciating days and nights. "She's offering a temp-to-perm contract with an option to hire you through her company after fifty business days."

"That's unbelievable!"

"I know! All you have to do is keep your nose clean for the next ten weeks and you'll land yourself one heck of a great position. FYI, I stand to earn a sizable finder's fee in the event they exercise your option, so try not to screw this up for either of us."

"I won't."

"I'm super proud of you, Ethan. Word is Cynthia took quite a shine to you."

"She's not so bad herself."

"Now that you mention it, I wanted to ask you about that. Is it true what they say about her, that she's a real looker?"

"You've never met her?"

"Haven't had the pleasure, though I've heard from various sources that she's quite an attractive specimen."

"She's all right, I guess," I respond, eager to hang up the phone and masturbate.

Later that evening, I meet my old high school buddies Seth and Teddy at Grandma's House, a run-down, dimly lit bar in Allston furnished like a stereotypical grandmother's living room, complete with lumpy sofas, brass floor lamps, and frayed Oriental carpets. We sit around a glass coffee table drinking pitchers of cheap beer while surreptitiously eyeing packs of Boston College girls dressed in tank-tops, tight shorts, and baseball caps. They drink and laugh, drink and laugh, as if programmed to run on a permanent loop. Not a single one of these girls can possibly be older than nineteen or twenty; there's no way they got past the bouncer without a fake ID. But on this night, for perhaps the first time in my adult life, I'm immune to their charms. My thoughts are running in another direction.

What's the harm in falling in love with Cynthia Rhodes? Not her *specifically*; she's married to just the sort of person I wouldn't want to have as an enemy. But why not someone *like* her, in her mid-thirties, hardened by experience, tough as nails?

"The chicks here are incredible!" Teddy blurts out, breaking my concentration.

"Did you see the blonde in the red tank-top at the bar?" Seth wants to know.

"White cut-off denim shorts?" Teddy asks.

"That's the one," Seth says. "Did you see her, Ethan?"

"Must have missed her," I lie.

"Jesus," Teddy says, "how could you have missed her? She has tits the size of cantaloupes."

"I'll be sure to keep a lookout," I say, without a trace of sincerity.

"What the hell is wrong with you?" Teddy shouts. "You used to love this place."

"Maybe I've outgrown it," I assert. "Half the girls in here aren't even twenty-one yet."

"You say that like it's a bad thing," Teddy jokes, cracking himself up as soon as the words leave his mouth.

"Shouldn't we at least be *trying* to meet girls our age?" I propose. "Christ, we're *twenty-six*."

"Hold on a second," Seth chimes in. "Now you're pissing me off too, so I'm gonna need to set you straight. Rewind the tape about eight or nine years, all the way back to high school, when every girl our age wanted to date a college guy—you remember those days, don't you? We were so jazzed to be in their shoes one day. But flash forward a couple years after that to when *we* were in college. Suddenly, everyone started talking about how gross it was to date high school girls. And all the chicks our age who we were *supposed* to be dating all of sudden started taking an interest in *older* guys who had already graduated college and landed shitty jobs. Okay, flash forward again, to right this very minute, and, guess what, Ethan, now *we're* the older guys with the shitty jobs. And wouldn't you know it, every girl our age has changed their tune yet *again,* and is on the hunt for some rich older dude to settle down with. So I've got bad news for you, Ethan: the twenty-six-year-old hotties we've been dreaming about, the ones our age with master's degrees in international diplomacy who speak fluent Italian and roll their own sushi, are off the market. They're either married, engaged, or holding out for the right guy, with the right IQ, the right family, and the right bank account. So don't get me started about girls our age, because they sure as hell ain't interested in us."

"What if you're wrong about that?" I argue.

"Trust me," Seth continues, "stop wasting your time chasing after girls in their twenties, or, God forbid, older. Find yourself a cute little hottie like the one over there with the cantaloupe tits. What do you think that girl sees when she looks over in our direction? I'll tell you what she sees—three handsome, clean-cut, grown-ass men with salaries, cars, and cool apartments, that's what."

"She ought to have her eyes checked," I shoot back.

"Come to think of it," Teddy reflects, "I may have to side with Ethan on this one. Hate to break it to you, man, but if that chick over there ever *did* bother to look in our direction—which is highly doubtful in the first place—all she'd see are a bunch of sad losers hanging out at a college bar they've clearly outgrown, trying desperately to get laid."

"Yeah, well, it's hard to argue with that," Seth admits, and we all laugh.

"Speaking of shitty jobs," I say, eager to change the subject, "I may have actually found one. I might even keep it for a while."

"No more temping?" Teddy asks, incredulous.

"I'll drink to that," Seth says. "Congrats."

"What kind of work is it?" Teddy wants to know.

"I don't want to oversell it—it's the same old administrative assistant, clerical bullshit I've been doing since graduation. But it's at a high-priced motivational speaking firm, and the best part about it is that my boss is a total fox."

"No shit. How old is she?" Seth asks.

"I'm not sure yet. Mid-thirties, I'm guessing. However old she is, she's unbelievably gorgeous, I'll tell you that. She puts all the girls here to shame."

"Married?" Teddy asks.

"Unfortunately, yeah. As a matter of fact, I know her husband too. He's old enough to be her father, and rich enough to cause me plenty of trouble."

"And how do you know all of this?" Teddy wonders.

"Because, up until a few days ago, I was working for *him*," I answer.

"That's pretty fucked up," Seth says. "You need to forget about that hot boss of yours and go after one of these college babes instead."

* * * *

I put on khakis and a button-down shirt and race out of my basement apartment worried I'll be late for my first official day at Hendrick and Lambert. Cynthia is already behind her desk in her private office when I tap on her door. "Good," she says, "we can get started."

Over the next several hours she familiarizes me with the computer network, the printers, assorted passwords, and her elaborate filing system, touching my arms and shoulders often as she patiently instructs me in soft, muted tones. Later, she leads me on a tour of the fifteenth floor, where I'm introduced to Joe Blow 1 and Joe Blow 2, star motivational speakers, along with a series of casually dressed sales associates, a bevy of overweight women from the accounting department, college interns whose only job appears to be stuffing brochures into envelopes, and a whole slew of middle-aged secretaries reeking of too many cigarettes. I meet close to thirty people, shaking hands and smiling awkwardly as Cynthia makes effortless small talk with each and every one of them. Once we've completed our rounds, Cynthia sits atop the metal desk in my outer office and sighs. "I'm famished," she says. "Let's ditch this shithole."

I follow her like an obedient child to a café a few blocks from our building, where she orders a grilled chicken Caesar salad and a large iced tea.

"I'll have the same," I tell our waitress.

"What's your impression so far?" Cynthia asks me.

"Well, to be honest, I'm still a little confused."

"How so?"

"Usually I can figure out one of these assignments within a matter of hours. But this place is kind of a mystery to me. I just met two motivational speakers—not five, not ten, but *two*—plus another *thirty* people who seemed pretty damn busy considering they're not being asked to motivate anyone."

She laughs. "Just follow my lead and you'll be fine."

"All right then."

"I was *kidding*," she says. "Fuck! Why would you follow my lead without questioning me first?"

"I don't know. Sorry."

"I'll try to explain it, but it's boring as shit so you'll need to tell me shut up once you've heard enough. The motivational speaking, that's icing on the cake. Those two dipshits you met would be standing in an empty auditorium with their dicks in their hands if it were up to them. What you don't see is all the machinery keeping the whole operation afloat. And what you *really* don't see is all the convoluted bullshit that forms the basis of our entire business model. All we're interested in when it comes right down to it are client retainers and selling books. Everything else is gravy."

I shrug, but I have no idea what Cynthia's talking about.

"Hang on, do you really care about what it is we're selling?" she asks.

"I mean, yeah, I guess I do."

"Fine, but don't say I didn't warn you. Let's say you're a mid-level exec at a Fortune 500 company in charge of two dozen pathetic losers in a chronically underperforming department. Your team is made up of a bunch of whining, demoralized, passive-aggressive *assholes*, and half of them are five minutes away from getting shit-canned or reassigned. Well, guess what, you and your team are the perfect suckers—I mean *candidates*—to spend 48 hours locked in a hotel conference room with one of our so-called expert facilitators to improve your department's efficiency and morale."

I nod in agreement, but it sounds even shadier than what her husband was up to at Boston Prop.

"Every corporation these days is looking for a competitive edge," she goes on, "and motivational speaking is a hot growth industry. Bob Hendrick and Ken Lambert, the founders, got into this racket by writing a god-awful, putrid book that's been on the best-seller list for ten years and counting. I can't imagine you've heard of it."

"What's it called?"

"*Shut Up and Listen.*"

"Is that the title, or are we doing an Abbott and Costello routine?"

"It's the title," she says, biting into a piece of chicken. (She's right, by the way—I've never heard of it.)

More bites of salad, more sips of iced tea. She continues: "We charge gobs of money to teach dumb, lazy fuck-ups how to find meaning in the mundane, soul-crushing tasks they perform each and every day of their miserable lives. We feed them enough regurgitated Eastern philosophy and New Age, self-help, fairy-tale bullshit to convince them that, whenever they send a fax or write a memo, they're in fact participating in some grand cosmic experiment. Afterwards, the participants are so absorbed in their own personal transformative journeys that most of them will report a significant increase in job satisfaction when surveyed."

I have no idea how to respond, decide I'm better off keeping my mouth shut.

"I wish I could tell you why I stick around this place," she confides. "It's a waste of my goddamned talents, that's for sure. It took me years to figure this out, but it turns out what we're *really* selling are insurance policies. Yeah, insurance. Corporations live in constant fear these days that their best and brightest employees will become so sad and deranged that they'll end up bringing automatic weapons to work with them. That happens more often than you'd like to think. If Hendrick and Lambert can keep one disgruntled pencil pusher from opening fire in the middle of a staff meeting, then maybe we've done some good."

It occurs to me this might've been relevant information to have before I accepted the job—though, given my current feelings for Cynthia, I doubt it would've made much of a difference.

She picks every last morsel of chicken and romaine from her plate, leaving behind two tomato slices that had no business being there in the first place (I ate mine). "After I married Linden," she says, twirling her fork, "I thought it would be a good idea to keep one foot planted in the workforce. I didn't want to turn into one of those Beacon Hill ladies who lunch, you know what I mean? Now it's just a huge pain in my ass. Speaking of pains in my ass, I should probably warn you about Bob and Ken, the partners."

"Warn me?"

"When a company hires Hendrick and Lambert Consulting to turn around a failing division, they're paying big bucks for the brilliant iconoclasts, Bob and Ken. In reality, those two deviants will show up for a kickoff meeting over coffee and bagels before hightailing it over to their country club for eighteen holes of golf. God only knows what they're doing when they're not playing golf. You wouldn't believe the types of expenses I've had to bury over the years. Come to think of it, it's probably best if we don't get into any of *that*."

"Yeah, maybe save that story for another day," I volunteer.

"They're *notorious* womanizers, those two, burning through tens of thousands of dollars of company revenue on high-priced escorts every goddamned year. Wow, I can't believe I just told you that."

"I can't believe you did either."

"I'd like to say they haven't pulled any of that sleazebag shit on me..."

"Do you mean —"

"Did they try to get me into bed with them, Ethan? Is that what you want to know? Did either of those two *degenerates* proposition me since I've been working at the company? Take a wild guess."

"But they can't do that. They're the founders. Their names are on the door."

She looks away, shaking her head. "I can't decide whether you're naive or just plain stupid," she finally says. "They haven't tried anything in the past couple of months, in case you're concerned for my well-being. I must finally be too old for those two creeps."

"Come on!" I shout back, offended for her.

"What, you think I'm lying? I'm over the hill, as far as men like that are concerned."

"How is that possible? You're so...young."

"Seriously, Ethan, if you insist on kissing my ass every minute, I'm gonna call Donna the second we get back to the office and have her send me over someone else."

"Maybe they decided to leave you alone out of respect for you as a married woman," I say, my voice cracking.

Cynthia's mouth drops open in seeming disbelief. "Please tell me you're not suggesting those two horndogs are deterred by the fact that they play golf with my *husband*?"

She laughs so hard that a sizable chunk of lettuce shoots out of her mouth and lands in her iced tea, and now we're both laughing.

"Oh my God, what fucking planet are you from?" she says. "I'm at least a decade past my expiration date to guys like Bob and Ken."

No woman has ever spoken to me like this before. It's exhilarating.

"It's not all bad," she assures me. "There are plenty of perks. I've trained everyone around the office to keep their distance, and you'll be right by my side each step of the way. We're gonna have a blast, you and me. Let me ask you a question," she says, her voice noticeably warmer. "Separate topic. Why are you still living in this godforsaken, buttoned-up, walking inferiority complex of a city, when you could've bought a bus ticket at any moment and gotten the fuck out?"

"Oh, you don't want to hear about that," I tell her.

"Hey, shit-for-brains," she says, throwing a balled-up napkin at my face, "in case you haven't figured it out yet, I want to hear about *everything*."

*   *   *   *

I graduated UMass in 1988 with a degree in English that was, already then, comically impractical. The nearly two thousand dollars remaining in my checking account —courtesy of a dead uncle—served to blunt defeats I felt certain were headed my way, while a still virginal BayBank credit card with a one thousand dollar credit limit consoled me only to the degree that, for a brief period at least, it would be mathematically impossible to fall into debt.

During my final weeks of school, my older brother Andy, who rented an apartment in nearby Springfield, was on the lookout for an affordable used car that could survive the cross-country trip to Los Angeles I was planning to take after graduation. My parents, aware of my intentions, were fiercely opposed, though not enough to prevent me from going through with it. I pitched the trip to them as a kind of extended summer vacation, a reconnaissance mission, purely exploratory, and as soon as they began referring to my plans as something I needed to "get out of my system," I knew they wouldn't stand in my way.

My brother and I, in those days, could hardly be described as close. While we may not have been actively at war with each other anymore, we weren't exactly on speaking terms either. But I needed a car, and Andy's priorities—he had a clear preference for engines over people—for one brief moment overlapped with mine. Andy narrowed down several potential options in the Amherst area before riding to campus on his motorcycle —its carburetor modified to let out a deafening scream —to pick me up. He brought with him an extra helmet and a folded copy of the *Want Ads*, and I had little choice but to wrap my arms around his waist and hold on for dear life.

We tooled around Amherst on his Harley, checking out old V-6's and V-8's. Andy maintained that, as far as engines were concerned, Fords were the best. I reminded him that Henry Ford had been a virulent anti-Semite, but Andy dismissed my concerns. "You need a car," he groaned. "Defend the Jews on your own time." We settled on a 1979 sky blue Ford Fairmont with extensive rust damage and 90,000 miles on its odometer.

Andy inspected its engine for over an hour before giving it his seal of approval. He deemed the car "solid," "a workhorse," and "one hell of a piece of machinery," but I wasn't so sure. Nevertheless, it had an upgraded cassette deck and speaker system, which clinched the deal for me, since I'd be the one driving the damn thing three thousand miles across the country. I handed the owner five hundred dollars in cash, and, by the end of the following week, Andy had replaced the carburetor, starter, and alternator in his garage back in Springfield. Within days of tossing my cap into the air at my predictably underwhelming UMass graduation ceremony, I was cutting through the Berkshires, heading west.

I'd read my share of Kerouac and couldn't wait to channel a bit of Sal Paradise on my trip west. Instead, I received automated wake-up calls each morning at 8:00 a.m. sharp before checking out of another Motel 6 and merging onto whatever interstate got me across the middle part of the country as efficiently as possible. I spent ten hours each day behind the wheel, listening to the same half dozen Elvis Costello and Joe Jackson cassettes over and over again. I'd sing along at the top of my lungs—I knew every lyric by heart—on my way to yet another Motel 6 (paid for with my brand new credit card), which I'd aim to reach by sundown. One night, for kicks, I pulled into a truck stop to take a quick nap in my car, but that was about as crazy as things got. I paid for gas, meals, and motels with plastic, even using my credit card to phone my parents from my motel rooms each night to let them know I was still alive. As much as I tried, I couldn't picture a modern-day Sal Paradise phoning his parents before going to bed at night, or, for that matter, charging the call to his credit card.

And then I arrived—Los Angeles, early June, 1988. Andy had been spot-on about the Ford: it got me west without a hint of trouble, and before I knew what hit me I was stopping at red lights for the first time in a week, marveling at the way street signs were featured so prominently at all the intersections. I had a map at the ready in the passenger seat, but hardly needed it: you could follow the same street for miles and miles and it would take you in a straight line. That may not sound like a big deal to most people, but try doing that in Boston.

I cut through the city to the Fairfax District—North Hayworth Avenue, to be precise—where a guy I knew from high school offered to let me crash on his sofa for a few nights. He'd moved to L.A. to try to make it as an actor, but was currently subsisting on peanut butter sandwiches and Top Ramen. He had the most uncomfortable couch I'd ever slept on, and, once I found a place of my own, I found no reason to speak with him ever again.

The apartment where I eventually landed was miles from Fairfax, in Westwood, spitting distance from

U.C.L.A. Back at UMass, a teaching assistant had given me what turned out to be shrewd advice: upon arrival in Los Angeles, head over to the student union on the U.C.L.A. campus to find listings from undergrads desperate to sublet their apartments before they left town for the summer.

Sure enough, every bulletin board in and around the student union was papered with ads for summer sublets. There were dozens of options to choose from, the majority priced under two hundred dollars a month (the only catch was that you had to pay for the whole summer up front). I settled on a three-bedroom, fully furnished unit in a relatively modern six-floor apartment building on Kelton Avenue, with air conditioning, wall-to-wall carpeting, a high-end stereo system, a VCR, cable television with a subscription to HBO, and a stationary bicycle. All three of the roommates who shared the unit had, at the very last minute, decided to get away from Los Angeles that summer, which meant I'd have their entire furnished apartment to myself until the end of August.

I spent most of those early days lounging around my chilled, carpeted oasis, where I took thirty minute showers and lay on the couch in my underwear to watch cheesy action movies on HBO. Each morning, I'd stroll the few blocks to the nearest *Los Angeles Times* vending machine to find out if the Red Sox had won their previous game or not. That summer, the Sox got off to a slow start before making a run at the pennant, and I'd expend entire mornings studying box scores and batting averages, trying to decide whether my team stood any chance against the mighty Athletics.

I awoke one night craving a glass of milk. Switching on the kitchen light, I spotted at least a hundred bloated cockroaches scurrying for cover across the linoleum floor. In that instant, my stretch of perfect isolation had been obliterated; I'd been sharing the apartment with houseguests after all. The following morning, I bought three cans of roach killer and sprayed the kitchen indiscriminately at one-hour intervals for the remainder of the day. I went through so much pesticide that I couldn't as much as step into the kitchen without my sneakers sticking to the linoleum. When the cans were emptied, I rushed back to the store for more.

As night fell, I turned off all the apartment lights and sat quietly at the dining room table, hoping to lull the cockroaches into a false sense of security. When enough time had passed—and I'd worked up the necessary courage—I switched the kitchen lights back on and stomped to death as many of the disgusting creatures as I could get to before their more fortunate comrades managed to slip away behind appliances and cabinetry. I repeated this procedure on three successive nights, before tossing my sneakers—the instrument of so much unbridled killing—into the trash can. Every time I flicked on the kitchen lights from that point on, there were no cockroach left to crush.

I'd come to California to fulfill a promise I'd made to myself in college (it was the closest thing I had in those days to ambition). Put simply, I felt compelled to write a screenplay in an L.A. apartment with a cigarette lodged between my lips. The smoking part came easily enough (though it's harder than you might think to keep a lit cigarette in your mouth without getting smoke in your eyes), while the writing of an actual screenplay proved the much greater challenge. I had no desktop computer, no training in the mechanics of screenwriting, and hardly a single decent idea for a movie. I ended up filling stacks of legal pads with aimless musings instead.

That was how I envisioned the rest of my summer would go—filling up legal pads with pseudo-profound insights, eating deli meat sandwiches, pouring over box scores in the newspaper, and riding the stationary bike every once in a while for exercise—until Mackenzie Pierson, one of the roommates supposedly out of town until the end of August, returned to the apartment unannounced. Craving my seclusion after a hard fought battle with hordes of repulsive insects, and wearing only my underwear, I was sprawled out on the living room sofa when Mackenzie stepped through the door. "Jesus Christ!" she shrieked, dropping her luggage as soon as she caught sight of me on her couch.

I'd been isolated for too long, murdered too many cockroaches, and for all I know could have been hallucinating from traces of bug spray still flowing through the air; whatever the reason, I became convinced the girl standing in front of me was addressing me by name, that *I* was Jesus Christ. I took a moment to remind myself that I was Jewish and didn't believe in Jesus, and that seemed to do the trick. Several seconds passed before it dawned on me that I was lying on a stranger's couch in my underwear.

That's when I screamed too. I bolted past her to my bedroom, slamming the door behind me and hiding under my blanket like a little kid during a thunderstorm. Complicating matters, I had no idea whether the bedroom I'd chosen to sleep in these past few weeks in fact belonged to the girl presently standing in the living room—though a quick scan of the collection of Brian De Palma movie posters on the walls suggested otherwise. Mackenzie, laughing hysterically outside my door, introduced herself and apologized for not phoning in advance. All I could think of was that I was the cockroach now and she'd switched on the lights.

Mackenzie was a year away from completing her undergraduate degree in Communications. Her travel plans had fallen through, and she and I would be stuck with each other for the remainder of the summer. It wasn't long before I discovered that she couldn't stand to be alone. Nothing felt more unnatural to her than spending more than five minutes by herself.

We shopped for groceries together, went to the movies twice a week (you couldn't walk half a block in Westwood without tripping over a movie theater), and made day trips in my rusted-out Fairmont to Zuma Beach, the Venice Boardwalk, and Third Street Promenade. She hated to cook, and insisted that we eat the majority of our breakfasts, lunches, and dinners at dive restaurants around the neighborhood. When we weren't jamming noodles and thinly sliced chicken into plastic bowls at the Mongolian Barbecue place on Gayley, we were devouring chili cheeseburgers at Tommy's, just down the street. I wouldn't have done any of this had Mackenzie not been my constant companion. I wouldn't even have known those places existed.

A physical relationship between us didn't appear to be in the cards. That's not to say I didn't fantasize about it. Mackenzie was in terrific shape; she had an athlete's slim, tanned body. She also happened to be the only girl I knew in the entire state of California— though if I'd met another twenty, I doubt I would've picked any of them over Mackenzie. But my interest in her went unreciprocated. One night, she stumbled home drunk with a guy she'd met at a party, and they disappeared into her bedroom to have sex. What I learned about Los Angeles apartment buildings that night was that you can't assume the walls will provide any sound-proofing whatsoever. It took Mackenzie more than an hour to reach orgasm, but not for lack of trying. She kept giving the poor guy specific instructions on how to use his tongue and fingers to speed up the process, but somehow none of it seemed to translate into tangible results. Her subdued climax, after fits and starts, was no doubt a well-earned victory for the both of them.

All the while, what was once a two thousand dollar bank balance at the start of my summer had dwindled down to zero, and I needed to find a source of income if I had any chance of staying on past August. Mackenzie, never one to hold back her opinion, urged me to cut my losses and return home. Instinctively, she sensed that I didn't belong in Los Angeles and never would. Here's how she put it: living in L.A. was like having to sit through an endless joke without ever reaching the punchline. I never did figure out what she meant be that, though it might have had something to do with the idea that Angelenos aren't too keen on laughing at themselves. And they don't much care for criticism about their city either: if a native Angeleno ever catches a whiff of condescension on your breath, they invariably revert to a defensive posture.

Mackenzie boasted about being able to navigate in and out of the L.A. mindset on account of her parents' divorce. Growing up, she'd spent half the year with her father outside Philadelphia and the other half with her mother in Tarzana. While on the East Coast, she'd proclaim her distaste for everything Hollywood—a necessary survival skill—until she could return to L.A. at last and gleefully erase all remnants of Philadelphia from her consciousness.

I'm not sure why I didn't try harder to have a relationship with Mackenzie. I must've been in awe of her, mesmerized by the way she glided so effortlessly across geographical and social boundaries. I couldn't even articulate to her what I was *doing* in L.A.—I'd stopped taking notes for my imaginary screenplay within days of her arrival. By the third week in August, as her two roommates were set to return, I hadn't even begun looking for a low-paying job or another place to live.

I'd driven clear across the country in the gas guzzler my brother had rescued from the scrap heap just to shadow a fearless twenty-year-old extrovert for two laid-back, dazzling months. We stocked our fridge with Rolling Rocks and California Coolers, survived on a steady diet of chili cheeseburgers and Mongolian barbecue, dropped acid once, listened to the same Everything But The Girl CD on repeat, and somehow never got around to falling in love. And when at last I ran out of money and time, I drove in the opposite direction on the very same highways that brought me to her. We said we'd keep in touch, but I already knew we wouldn't, and never even bothered to send her a postcard from Boston. Still, I'm more likely to misspell my middle name than fail to remember a single detail from the summer I spent as Mackenzie Pierson's accidental roommate.

* * * *

I'm now picking up Cynthia's line whenever it rings, answering each call the same way: "Cynthia Rhodes's office. How may I help you?" She receives more calls on a given day than any boss I've ever worked for; I'm not even allowed to use the bathroom without getting permission first. Most of these phone calls are work-related, but a significant number are from Cynthia's friends, all men. In short order I can distinguish her most frequent callers before they've even said their names. I'm under strict orders to transfer these calls, never taking a message, craning my neck just in time to watch Cynthia gently close her door before picking up the receiver. Once she's off the line and her office door swings open again, she can't wait to bend my ear, sharing intimate details with me about men who aren't her husband.

I haven't had the chance to meet too many married people. My parents, obviously (though I'm not sure that counts), along with all the couples in their vast circle of friends. I remember hearing about a handful of divorces among their group, but I'd have no way of knowing whether infidelity was the root cause. It's probably safe to assume that my *parents* never cheated on each other, but, then again, had my mother or father decided to be unfaithful, I'd be the last person to find out.

So when Cynthia talks to me about the men she's slept with in her past, or the men who desire to sleep with her *still*, it usually takes a few seconds for me to register what she's saying. She's *married*. She should *not* be speaking of such things. Listen, I'm no prude, nor am I in denial about couples having sex outside of marriage; I've just never met anyone so eager to discuss it.

Men proposition her constantly. Just one example would be the rich attorney who offers to fly her down to the Bahamas for a weekend of "repeated fucking." Whenever I transfer this guy's calls, Cynthia lets out a hearty laugh and screams out, "he must be horny again!" —though it's never entirely clear from her reaction what she plans to do about it. But there are many, many others. There's an ex-boyfriend—let's call him Ex-A, as he's one of several exes she still keeps in touch with—a frequent lunch date who believes "all women are insane" and takes no responsibility whatsoever for his multitude of failed relationships. "He's desperate to fuck me," Cynthia confides, "but the asshole makes my skin crawl." Then there's Ex-B, a total loser who coaches girls' high school basketball and cheats on his wife shamelessly, often with his students. Gross.

I should also mention her notorious ex-fiancé, a man who got cold feet a few weeks before their long-planned wedding, famously breaking the whole thing off and sending Cynthia into a panic. Cynthia enjoys retelling this story; it's easily her favorite. Her ex-fiancé remains to this day flabbergasted by Cynthia's subsequent decision to marry Mr. Rhodes; he calls the office at least twice every week, pleading for a second chance. Cynthia feels a mixture of contempt and pity for him, but takes his calls regardless.

The only man I never seem to hear from is Mr. Rhodes himself. I can't imagine what he must think of me, or if he even remembers my name. Nearly a month passes before I get my answer.

"Cynthia Rhodes's office," I recite for the tenth time that morning. "How may I help you?"

"If it isn't the one and only Ethan Gill."

"Mr. Rhodes!"

"Cynthia tells me you've been doing damn near impeccable work. That's quite an endorsement, coming from her. She's no easy woman to please."

"A job isn't worth doing unless it's done right," I say, quoting his own words back to him.

"You were listening after all! You're sorely missed around these parts, Ethan. Shirley's been taking her sweet time getting back, and your replacement is a lousy conversationalist. Sebastian misses you too. He hasn't killed anything in weeks."

"He'll snap out of it."

"Keep up the good work, young man. You can go ahead and transfer me now."

"Will do," I say, placing him on hold. "Cynthia, your husband's on the line."

"What does the old fart want?" she laughs. "Take a message, will ya?"

Cynthia's office is twice the size of mine, with a lovely view of the city and harbor—yet she still prefers passing multiple hours each day in my cramped, windowless outer office instead. After she's done jabbering away on her telephone, she'll usually reserve a few hours at the end of each day to spend with me, leaning against my metal desk, demanding my full attention.

She expects absolute transparency from me, and I aim to never disappoint. I'm an open book when it comes to my personal life anyway; Cynthia just happens to be the only person interested in reading it.

And yet, no matter how desperately I thirst for her understanding, I remain inhibited in her presence, displaying a bashfulness that hampers my ability to communicate more freely. She's so beautiful that it's sometimes a challenge to keep eye contact with her for prolonged stretches. This may sound corny as hell, but her face is a bit like the sun: you can't stare at it directly or it'll burn your retinas. Also, she likes to talk *dirty*. And I don't just mean that every other word out of her mouth is *fuck this* or *fuck that*. It goes far beyond that. Men are always trying to fuck her with their *hard, stupid cocks,* which is an insane thing to hear from a gorgeous woman, let alone someone who's your boss.

But my reticence is short-lived, and in no time I'm spilling the beans—and not just about my summer in Los Angeles with Mackenzie. I'm essentially recounting my entire life story, keeping Cynthia entertained with silly anecdotes about my European, intellectual parents, my perpetually horny friends, and my older brother Andy, a security guard now, married and living somewhere in the woods of New Hampshire.

Naturally, Cynthia couldn't care less about any of that boring crap. All she wants to hear about is my sex life.

There's a certain trajectory to our conversations. They generally don't get underway until late in the day, after she's joined me in the outer office and closed the door leading out to the hallway.

"What's your longest relationship?" she demands to know on one such occasion.

"It lasted about three months, which was twice as long as my previous record."

"Did she have a name?"

"Stephanie. I met her at a bar. She was tall, with sharp cheekbones, and long, straight hair, sort of strawberry blond. After she broke up with me, I heard through the grapevine that she was anorexic."

"You weren't able to figure that out on your own?"

"God no. She used to pick at her french fries at restaurants, but I never suspected a thing."

"Apart from the eating disorder, what else can you tell me about her?"

"Well, she'd never seen a Stanley Kubrick movie, which I thought was extremely bizarre. So we rented *The Shining* before we did it for the first time."

"How was it?"

"The movie or the sex?"

"The movie I know. Tell me about the sex."

"It was okay."

"Just okay?"

"I wasn't blown away by it, if that's what you mean. I'm never blown away by it. Come to think of it, sex and *The Shining* aren't too dissimilar—that is, you want to know what all the fuss is about, but it turns out they're both a little overrated."

She looks at me for quite some time after that.

"You think sex is overrated?" she asks, finally.

"I guess so, yeah."

"Has it occurred to you that you might be doing it wrong?"

"Sure, but how am I supposed to fix it? I'm no authority when it comes to that stuff."

She nods.

"What about you?" I ask, blushing.

"What *about* me? You want to know if I'm good at fucking?"

"What? Jesus —"

"Well, that *is* what you were asking, right?"

"I swear to God it wasn't."

"I'll let it slide," she says, looking away. "I wish it were that simple. Good in bed, bad in bed—that's not really a distinction I concern myself with these days."

"Doesn't that kind stuff matter to you?"

"Sex isn't like tennis, Ethan. You don't just get better at it with practice."

"Great. That might just be the worst news I've heard all year."

"You're missing my point," she says, laughing and punching me softly on my shoulder. "Sure, if you did it as often as I have, you'd pick up a few pointers along the way. And yeah, you might even improve at it, but that wouldn't necessarily make it any better."

"Now I'm even more confused."

"Get back to me in ten years," she says. "It'll make more sense to you then."

On a different day, she wants to hear about how I lost my virginity.

"Oh, *that* story," I volunteer eagerly. "That's where it all went downhill for me." Like I said, open book.

A huge smile forms across her face.

"I was nineteen," I start. "I know, I know, super old. Second semester, freshman year. My brother, Andy, who was a real jerk to me at the time, would call me once a week to see if I'd gotten laid yet. It was unbelievably demoralizing. I was living in Southwest, the rowdiest section of UMass, where most the freshmen get placed. Everything my friends and I did in those days revolved around cheap beer and listening to Aerosmith. And every conversation was about one, and only one, topic: how we were gonna get laid. Each night it was the same routine: drink beer, listen to "Dream On," and argue about which girls in the dorm we would or wouldn't kick out of bed.

"A lot of us were taking the shuttle bus over to Smith College on weekends, hoping to score. That's an all-girls college, in case you didn't know, steeped in tradition—but to us it might as well have been a school for Martians. Compared to where we were living, the dorms over there looked like we had gone back in time a hundred years. There was antique furniture in the lobbies, oil paintings on the walls, that sort of thing. And the girls—not all of them, obviously, maybe not even half—seemed genuinely interested in getting to know us. And yes, I was aware even back then that a lot of them were probably lesbians, but that just made the whole experience more thrilling.

"Anyway, Smith girls would host these monster parties in the lounges of their dorms on Saturday nights, but you had to be on the guest list to be allowed in. The girls would be decked out in fancy cocktail dresses, expensive jewelry, stuff like that. You had to see it to believe it. And these rich guys from Amherst College and as far away as Harvard and Dartmouth would show up in their navy blazers and yellow ties. It was surreal. My friends and I, who were never officially on any guest list, perfected a foolproof method for getting through the door. A group of us would huddle near the entrance while this one guy, cool as a cucumber, would go inside and sneak a peek at the guest list and memorize a name. Then we'd wait about five minutes and all arrive together, and one of us would mention the name and we'd all get waved past security. It worked like a charm.

"I'll never forget those parties. Free drinks. And not just beer, but white Russians, whiskey sours, gin and tonics. We got drunk as hell, and Christ did we dance. It sure was something to see. The girls were altogether different from the types we were used to at UMass. They were shy, reserved, some with voices so soft you almost had to lean in to hear them. Your typical pretty girl at UMass might try to verbally assassinate you if you dared strike up a conversation with her at a party, but these Smith girls were nothing like that. They were just as good-looking as the UMass girls—prettier even—but they were demure. They were the epitome of demure. You almost felt guilty trying to score with them. I mean, here we were, a bunch of horny freeloaders who weren't even supposed to *be* there, and these girls were eager to dance with us, handing us mixed drinks, engaging us in conversation, giving us the time of day. It was crazy."

"Yeah, yeah," Cynthia chimes in. "Get to the good stuff already."

"Right, sorry. So there was this one girl, her name was Aubrey. She'd just had her hair bobbed, if you can believe it, just like Bernice in that Fitzgerald short story."

Cynthia shrugs. "Not familiar with the reference. *This* story, on the other hand, is getting on my nerves."

"Aubrey was shy and *extremely* cute. We'd been dancing together for about five songs before I got the nerve to make a move. Can we skip over this part?"

"*This* is the part you want to skip over? Jesus Christ."

"Fine." Deep breath. "So there we were, scandalizing her dorm-mates, French kissing in the middle of the dance floor. Afterwards, we went outside for a quick stroll, which led to more French kissing, which sooner or later led us back to her dorm room. Oh, I need to explain something about the dorms at Smith."

"Please don't."

"Wait, this is *important*. All the students there get their own private dorm rooms. Can you believe that?"

"Astonishing."

"Okay, okay. So there I was, basically living out my college fantasy. You have to understand, Smith girls were like the Holy Grail to my group of friends. Every guy I knew dreamed of getting lucky with a Smith girl. Things were getting pretty hot and heavy on her bed, and all the while Aubrey was telling me this sob story about having just broken up with some Ivy League douchebag. She was going on and on about how she was afraid of dating another asshole who might break her heart, blah blah blah, how she didn't want anything like that to happen to her again anytime soon. I'm guessing I must've promised I'd never do that, blah blah blah, that I wasn't the sort of person who'd do that to a girl. So we're on her bed, our clothes coming off fast, kissing like it's the end of the world, when she whispers something about being on her period. She tells me that, when we have sex, I might see a little blood down there and would that be okay. I just kept kissing her and kissing her...Can we *please* skip over this part?"

"We cannot," Cynthia says.

"Next thing I know, she disappears into the bathroom to put in her diaphragm. Oh, hang on, I forgot to mention another important detail. Not only do girls at Smith live in their own single dorm rooms, but they have their own private bathrooms too!"

"I'm blown away by the details you find important. Get to the sex already!"

"So now she's speaking to me from inside her bathroom while putting in her diaphragm. She's explaining that it was the second day of her period but you can never be too careful. Meanwhile I'm just sitting there, on the edge of her bed, waiting. And next thing I know I'm starting to think about what it would feel like to finally lose my virginity. My brother was sure to call me up in a few days to see if I'd gotten laid yet, and *this* time I'd finally be able to tell him that I had. Yes, goddammit, you stupid jerk, your little brother got laid! But then something else started kicking around inside my brain. I can't fully explain it—it's like I could see into the future or something. I knew, just *knew*, with absolute certainty, that I wouldn't be able to have sex with this girl. That I wouldn't be able to get it up. What's funny is that I'd never gotten this close to having sex before. I mean, this girl was putting in her diaphragm in the next room! And sure enough, as soon as she got back to the bed and we were fooling around again, it was gone."

"Gone?"

"Totally gone. It wouldn't come back for anything."

"You *do* realize this was supposed to be a story about how you lost your virginity, right?"

"We lay in her bed together, and she assured me it didn't matter. But I was inconsolable—suicidal thoughts were racing through my brain. She fell asleep in my arms, but I couldn't sleep a wink. I literally stayed up all night, and, at the first hint of the sunrise, I said goodbye, promising to keep in touch. But I already knew I'd never speak to her again. I got away from that campus as fast as I could, but it was a Sunday, and the shuttle bus wasn't scheduled to run until much later that morning. I ended up walking all the way from Northampton to Southwest, and that's a hell of a walk, trust me, especially when you're contemplating suicide the entire time."

"That's it?" Cynthia snaps, "That's your story? You said goodbye to her and dragged your ass home? Oh my God, that's the saddest fucking thing I've ever heard in my entire life."

"There's more. I bragged to all my friends afterwards that we'd really done it. I became a *legend* in my dorm. And, sure enough, the next time my brother called, I lied to him about having sex as well. He was so proud of me, he sent me a box of cigars. I felt like the biggest fraud in the history of the universe. I didn't end up losing my virginity for real until about three months later, over summer vacation with some girl I met on a beach. The earth didn't move, I can tell you that. Not even close. It was over in about a minute. But the worst part was that I couldn't even talk to my friends about what it had felt like to lose my virginity, because, as far as they were concerned, I'd already been through that with Aubrey."

"How utterly devastating that must've been for you. I'm surprised you were able to carry on."

"Hey, it was a big deal at the time."

"Did you ever find out what happened to her?"

"Who, Aubrey? *No!* Weren't you listening? I never spoke with her again."

"That's a damn shame," Cynthia says. "She sounded like a real nice girl."

* * * *

I'm not sure how it works with most people, but, in my experience, if I'm putting a lot of attention into one area of my life, I end up letting the other parts slide.

Take my mother and father, for instance. We don't talk on the phone nearly as often as we once did, unless there's bad news to share. Ever since I moved out of their basement a few years back, I hardly speak to them at all. Months pass without a *visit*, in spite of the fact that they still live in the same Newton house where I grew up, just a few miles from my current apartment.

But they're still my parents, and, on the rare occasion I'm invited to their house for dinner, it's as if I'm obligated to go. They need to verify with their own eyes that I'm alive and well—not too skinny, not too fat. Their pretense for seeing me tonight is my father's seasonal leek soup, which he serves with a dollop of sour cream and sprigs of fresh chives in each bowl.

As soon as I'm through their front door, I'm bombarded with questions about my new boss. It's my first visit to their house since I started at Hendrick and Lambert, so their sudden interest in my life isn't a huge surprise; nonetheless, I'm not prepared for Cynthia to be the main topic of the evening's conversation. I do my best to recount our breezy, easygoing rapport, Cynthia's stunning beauty, her rebellious streak, as well as, as I describe it, the deep well of sadness that resides within her—all the while omitting key elements from my parents that might send the wrong message. I must be blushing, or beaming, or both, because, when I finish talking, my mother demands to know if I've fallen in love with Cynthia Rhodes.

"What? Are you nuts? Come on, Mom!"

"That's the distinct impression you're giving me."

"She's *married*," I stress. "I know her husband."

"Trust me, that makes no difference to a certain kind of woman. Mark my words, Ethan—she's dangerous, and you need to watch out for her."

I jump to Cynthia's defense. "A certain kind of woman? What exactly do you mean by that? Smart, sexy, honest—is that the kind of woman you're referring to?"

"She has no business being so chummy with you. Not only is she married, but she's your *boss*. She's obligated to maintain a professional distance. Back me up on this, Seymour."

"I'm still stuck on the whole *stunning beauty* aspect," my father says. "Would you mind painting a clearer picture of her? Maybe start by describing her figure in more detail. Would you say she's partial to dresses or skirts?"

I laugh.

"What's next?" my mother asks. "Dinner at her place? A movie? She sounds to me like a damaged soul. That's a recipe for disaster."

"Oh, I don't know about that," my father interjects. "All right, so she's beautiful—is that her fault? If we discriminated against every drop-dead gorgeous gal with emotional problems, where would we be as a society? I think Ethan's doing the right thing. He's making a new friend. That's important. He knows where to draw the line."

"Of course I do," I say. "Not in a million years would I let myself get involved with a married woman."

"You're already involved," my mother says.

"He means *sexually* involved," my father says. "He's promising to avoid becoming her lover."

"I know what he means," my mother says.

"Thanks for the support, Dad, but you should really stop using the word *lover*."

Come to think of it, I haven't seen much of my friends either. Over drinks one Saturday night, I receive a slightly different perspective on the matter of my new boss from Seth and Teddy.

"You need to fuck her on top of your metal desk," Seth insists.

"In my dreams," I say.

"I'm telling you," he continues, "that's what she wants! Trust me on this. She's dressing provocatively for a reason. It's only the two of you in that double office, alone for most of the day, am I right?"

"Pretty much."

"Then whatever outfit she's got on was chosen specifically for you."

"Nonsense," I say. "Her clothes are just a reflection of her personality. She's the type of woman who always wants to look attractive."

"What are you," Teddy barks, "her fucking *shrink*? How do you know why she does the things she does?"

"I just do, that's all. She's been objectified by men her whole life. It's practically second nature to her. She may not even be *aware* of half the signals she's sending out."

"Bullshit," Teddy says. "Complete and utter bullshit. You could see down her blouse that first day at your job interview, right?"

"So what?"

"Did you get an erection or didn't you?"

"You know I did."

"Which proves my point," he says, slamming the palm of his hand down on the table.

"And your point is?"

"She *let* you see down her blouse," Teddy shouts at me. "She *wanted* you to get an erection. And, unless I'm completely mistaken, she probably got a little wet watching it grow inside your pants."

"You're out of your goddamned mind," I tell him.

"Hang on, Ethan," Seth questions. "How would *you* know if she saw your boner or not? You were staring at her tits!"

"It wasn't like I could see her *actual* breasts," I clarify. "Mostly what I saw was her bra."

"And what about her nipples?" Teddy asks, deadly serious.

"What about them?"

"Could you see the shape of her nipples under her bra?"

I have to think about that one for a moment. "What difference does *that* make?" I respond.

"All the difference in the world," Teddy says, without elaborating.

I can't win with these guys. I say one thing, they hear another. "You *do* realize," I try one last time, "that not only is Cynthia married, not only would any relationship between the two of us be completely inappropriate, but she's a million times too beautiful to ever, ever, *ever* fall for a guy like me."

"You gotta drop the low self-esteem act once and for all," Seth says. "You and your ridiculous negativity. So what if she's hot? Maybe she sees something in you that she can't get from anyone else. Maybe she *likes* you— ever think of that? She opens up to you. She feels safe with you, precisely because you're *not* trying to cop a feel every minute of the day. You can *use* that. Take advantage of all that pathetic sensitivity of yours and *make a move!*"

"You're both crazy," I sigh, shaking my head.

"You and Cynthia, on the metal desk, fucking like rabbits," Teddy says, and we all laugh.

* * * *

As the weeks fly by, I resolve to pick up as many fragments as I can from Cynthia's past, chasing after pieces of her casually discarded biography as if they're clues in a scavenger hunt. I'd gladly trade ten of my own humiliating episodes in exchange for a single juicy morsel she's willing to divulge, knowing full well that any admission from Cynthia will dwarf all my depressingly lame stories put together. If Cynthia were the fictional character in an imaginary novel I'll never get around to writing (or possibly a screenplay, though I'd need to heighten the conflict for dramatic effect), I'd by this point in our relationship have collected enough background information to give her character what is referred to in screenwriting parlance as a "backstory" to explain her cynical attitudes and suggestive behavior. Key details from her life would be crystallized into an introductory chapter that might go something like this:

Cynthia Anne McKinnon was one of three children raised on the ground floor of a two-family clapboard house in Quincy, down the street from the church parking lot where she would ultimately lose her virginity at the age of fourteen. Her mother's side of the family, dirt poor and originally from Tennessee, relocated to Western Massachusetts during World War II to work at a weapons manufacturing plant in Springfield. Her father's side, like most everyone else in the neighborhoods around Quincy that Cynthia came to know so well, emigrated from Ireland in pursuit of a better life.

Cynthia's parents first met at a junior college in Worcester in 1957, where her mother was working toward a teaching certificate and her father was trying to decide whether or not the college had anything to teach *him*. They'd only been dating for about a month when they dropped out to get married. Cynthia's mother was already pregnant by then, and her father insisted on a return to Quincy, his old stomping grounds, where he would go on to open a television repair shop and earn enough from assorted broken appliances to support a wife and three children. Both parents, while still alive, are sickly and alcoholic, residing at the same address where they started out all those years ago. Cynthia, born in 1960, was the middle child, and the only girl. She tussled with her brothers often, twice landing in the emergency room with broken bones, having sought to prove herself as strong-willed and resilient as any boy.

Her mother was a Southern Baptist, her father a lapsed Catholic; consequently, Cynthia, to a large degree, avoided the requisite guilt and shame afflicting the majority of her friends. She kissed boys whenever the mood struck her, stayed out long past her curfew, and drank beer and wine with charismatic juvenile delinquents at the Quincy Quarries after dark. She kept a firm grip on her virginity as puberty set in, but by fourteen the pressure proved too great: her surrender, which may have been, in hindsight, too generous a term, took place in the cramped backseat of a red Dodge Omni with a sales associate from her father's shop, a man twice her age, in the aforementioned church parking lot around the corner from her house.

Her older brother joined the Marines after the Vietnam War was already over, but got wounded anyway (during military exercises in Thailand). He's a bartender in Everett now, wears an eye patch. Her younger brother quit high school to help out at their father's fledgling repair shop and proved instrumental in transitioning the business from televisions to desktop computers.

Cynthia enrolled at Northeastern University in the late '70s. Right off the bat, she discovered that she had a knack for calculus. She went on to become the first member of her family to earn an undergraduate degree, and had no trouble whatsoever finding work in the accounting departments of various Boston-area companies affiliated with her school's co-op program.

Trouble came from elsewhere.

The men she was attracted to and the men who were attracted to her all shared the same trait in common: they were consistently angry. About what Cynthia was never sure. For the longest time, it didn't occur to her that a person shouldn't have to put up with so much physical and emotional abuse. Rather, she took up jogging, moderated her drinking, and kept earning steady promotions at work. By her late twenties, after managing to extricate herself from one appalling relationship after another, she finally met a man she thought she could marry. There were plenty of warning signs that should have discouraged her—after waiting three years to propose, he insisted on a wedding date two more years down the line—but she blew right past those, unconcerned. When he eventually dumped her, it wasn't technically *at* the altar; it was a few weeks prior, at the bakery where the two of them were choosing the design for their wedding cake.

That's around the time Linden Rhodes entered the picture. He was night and day different from any man she'd ever known. The others had been oafish and crude (not to mention violent and stupid), whereas Mr. Rhodes was dignified and courteous, his world bursting with sophistication and privilege. He drank Scotch, not beer, was attired in pinstriped suits, not stained T-shirts. Twenty years her senior, he was the product of old money and a first-class education, and, twice divorced, recognized in Cynthia a measure of self-reliance and fearlessness severely lacking in his previous wives.

I'm afraid my introductory chapter would have to end there (besides, it would take someone a lot more talented than me to pull it off). Cynthia hasn't shared many details with me about how she came to meet Mr. Rhodes anyway, or what it's like to live in his Beacon Hill townhouse with a John Singer Sargent hanging on the living room wall.

It's left to me to fill in the gaps, and I choose to imagine Mr. Rhodes and Cynthia in separate bedrooms, keeping to themselves both physically and emotionally. It wouldn't surprise me one bit if Mr. Rhodes still kept the names of half a dozen high-priced call girls at the ready in his Rolodex, no doubt having come up with an ingenious way to get his company to pay for it.

* * * *

Needless to say, I learn next to nothing about motivational speaking during my time at Hendrick and Lambert, or even the full extent of Cynthia's responsibilities within the organization. Budget projections and expense reports make as little sense to me now as they did at the start. My confinement in Cynthia's office, sequestered from the rest of the company, is so complete that I often lose track of my fellow co-workers, and every so often need to remind myself that Cynthia and I are surrounded in every direction.

Without warning or fanfare, my fifty-day temp-to-perm contract comes to an abrupt end. The phone rings at my desk one morning, and, for perhaps the first time since I began at the company, the voice on the other end of the line is asking to speak to *me*.

Later that afternoon, I report to human resources, where associates I've never met before guide me through stacks of paperwork formalizing the terms of my employment and the particulars of my medical and dental benefits. I've never qualified for health insurance through an employer before. My previous eighty-dollar-a-month, out-of-pocket plan, with its five thousand dollar deductible, was as good as worthless. But that's all behind me now. Annual checkups: covered. Prescription drugs: covered. Biannual dental checkups and routine cleanings: covered. Annual optometrist visits: covered. Up to ten fifty-minute sessions with a mental health professional (should I be so inclined): covered. But that's not all. Yearly gym membership: subsidized. I even qualify for two full weeks of paid vacation and up to five sick days per year, not to mention paid time off for national holidays. Aren't there at least six or seven of those each year? That sounds about right. When combined with my vacation and sick days, that exceeds *twenty days* for which I'm to be paid to stay home. It feels almost too good to be true. I rush to the calculator for more surprises: I only need be physically present at Hendrick and Lambert two hundred and forty days per year (give or take), which, considering my close proximity to Cynthia, can hardly be considered much of a hardship at all.

Somehow, with minimal effort, I've accomplished the impossible: a clean escape from temp hell. No more time-sheets faxed to my employment agency at the end of each work week. No more unpaid lunch hours, unpaid sick days, unpaid holidays. No more second-rate health insurance plans with their outrageous deductibles. No more being referred to dismissively by every Tom, Dick, and Harry as "the temp." When Donna from the agency calls to congratulate me, I'm struck by the prospect that I may never have reason to speak with her again.

"Thanks a million," I tell her.

"Not at all," she says. "Remember that finder's fee we discussed? Guess who's taking a Caribbean cruise this winter?"

As the day winds down, Cynthia, perched on the edge of my metal desk and wearing one of her scandalously too-short skirts, offers to buy me a drink. "We absolutely must celebrate," she says. "Where should we go?"

I strain to appear composed. "You pick the place," I answer, staring intently at the folders on my desk.

"How about the Dusty Parrot?"

"Where's that?"

"Over by Faneuil Hall. You've probably walked past it a thousand times. Bland hamburgers, five varieties of

Sam Adams on tap, swarming with tourists and corporate stooges."

"Sounds like a nightmare. I'm in."

It's a short walk to Quincy Market from our building. Inside the busy restaurant, we're forced to navigate past a sea of middle-aged men in double-breasted suits just to reach the bar. It feels as if every guy in the place is taking turns flirting with Cynthia—though she doesn't seem to mind. On the contrary, she reciprocates the barrage of attention with a series of gestures, hair tosses, smiles, and giggles that imply gratitude. There's no question about it: Cynthia speaks fluent Male.

Just as I'm feeling certain that Cynthia is about to ditch me for someone with a better job, wardrobe, and haircut than mine (and, believe me, she'd have plenty of options in this place), she tugs on my shirt sleeve to remind me that I'm still alive.

"They can all fuck themselves," she whispers in my ear.

"Have you considered being a tad less encouraging to them?"

"Trust me, it wouldn't help."

We down foaming mugs of Samuel Adams (Octoberfest), our bodies virtually touching, pressed together by an after-work crowd that continues to swell inside the restaurant. Cynthia's wearing a particularly revealing outfit—the aforementioned miniskirt along with a flimsy purple blouse—and I steal glimpses of her lace bra each time I stare down at the mug I've positioned strategically near her elbow.

"I've been meaning to tell you something," she confesses.

Me too, I desperately want to tell her.

"Linden's in debt up to his eyeballs."

That wasn't what I was expecting to hear at all. "Yeah, right," I respond. "He's making a killing with those stupid REITs of his."

"I wish that were the case."

"Well, I'm sorry, but it *is,*" I insist. "I've personally inputted dozens of those coma-inducing contracts, one right after the other. I've seen the numbers."

"*Unsigned* contracts. And all those figures you saw were merely projections of future earnings. None of it was real."

"That's where you're wrong, Cynthia. I recorded wire transfers too. *Huge* numbers."

"Pass-through payments. Whatever microscopic commissions he managed to negotiate got vacuumed up by all the brokerage and property manager fees."

"That's *ridiculous,*" I protest. "The money's pouring in."

"No, it's not. It's an illusion. Linden's been living off his family's trust fund his entire life. Believe me, he's gone belly-up. Not only that, but the IRS is breathing down his neck. It's all about to crash down hard."

"*No*," I shout, growing upset for some unknown reason. "He wears Brooks Brothers suits! He belongs to half a dozen private clubs!"

"And I imagine his creditors won't take too kindly to any of that. It'll all come out in the audit."

"What are saying, Cynthia, that he's some kind of crook?"

"Please don't feel sympathy for Linden," she pleads with me, just loudly enough to be heard above the din. "That would just about break my heart."

"Okay," I promise, "I won't."

"Linden's guaranteed to land on his feet—that's kind of a specialty of his. The bulk of his fortune is safe, and by safe I mean that even *he* can't access it. Ages ago, his parents knew better than to entrust him with their inheritance in one lump payment, and a team of executors and lawyers have been a constant thorn in his side ever since. Not a single one of his properties is even in his *name*. The estate they set up for him is so well-guarded, not even the government can touch it. But make no mistake, one way or the other, Linden's days as a dick-swinging master of the universe are over."

I take a long sip of beer. "Jesus, Cynthia. I'm stunned."

"I wish that were the worst of it," she adds. "Any minute now, he'll be finished with me too."

It takes another few pints of beer for *that* to sink in, after which Cynthia insists on driving me home. We stumble in silence to the reserved parking garage where her black Jaguar sedan with tan leather seats is located. I'm too buzzed to get anywhere near a steering wheel, but Cynthia's apparently fine, expertly weaving in and out of heavy traffic on Storrow Drive while following my jumbled directions to my apartment in Allston. When we pull up to my building, she shuts off the engine and turns to me. "You'll find Linden's cigarettes in the glove compartment," she says. "I could use one right about now."

I locate a pack of Dunhills, hand them over.

"You smoke?" she asks.

"Camels, not these. But I guess there's a first time for everything."

She flicks ashes out the car window. "When he's through with me, I won't have a penny to my name."

"How do you know that?" I ask.

"It's all spelled out in the prenup. You might say I was just another three-year lease to him, not so different from the terms he got on this car."

And then she kisses me. There's still smoke in my lungs from my last drag on the Dunhill, but, without advance warning, there isn't any time to exhale. She pulls away a moment later, leaving me only a split second to get rid of that smoke before she's biting down hard on my lower lip. It's painful as hell, and yet, strangely, not the worst feeling in the world. I press my face against her cheek like I'm a character in one of those 1940s Hollywood melodramas, and, when we kiss again, I taste a hint of something metallic on her tongue, which I'm fairly confident is my own blood.

After another pause, she shoves me away with both hands, as if we've been in a fight.

"Now what?" I ask.

"I'm still trying to figure that out."

Again our lips meet, and, again, she draws blood. Out of the blue, a voice inside my head starts screaming at me, loud and clear, to suck on Cynthia's nipples through her purple blouse. I've never wanted anything so badly in my life. A split second later, one of her nipples is so engorged in my mouth that it threatens to poke a hole through the delicate fabric.

"Bite it," she says.

"What?"

"You heard me, Ethan."

I ignore her request and start sucking on her other perfect, hard nipple through the silk, creating two enormous wet spots on her blouse.

"Bite it or get lost," she says.

"Bite your nipple?"

"Did I stutter?"

"Because if you really want me to, I'll do it," I say.

"*Oh my God!*" she shouts at me, exasperated.

"Which nipple?" I ask her. "Do you have a preference?"

"For crying out loud, Ethan—*pick* one!"

I bite down on the left one—or is it my right and her left?

"Harder," she says. "'Til it bleeds."

No, I decide. That's where I draw the line. I already did what she asked of me—I bit the damn nipple—and I'm not about to break her skin. Ignoring her instruction, I lift her blouse over her chest and begin to massage her breasts instead.

"No, goddammit, no. *Bite it*," she repeats, "*'til it bleeds!*"

I loosen her bra, revealing breasts so flawless I've got no business being this close to them, much less cupping them in my trembling hands. The nipple I decide to concentrate on seems microscopically larger than the other one. Encircling it with my lips and tongue, I enlist all manners of trickery to avoid using my teeth—but that's not what she wants.

"Bite it."

"No."

"Bite it or get the fuck out."

"Fine. Jesus."

"Harder!" she screams, writhing in pain.

"I can't," I shoot back, "that's *enough*."

"'Til it bleeds," Cynthia says, her voice so agitated now she's nearly hissing.

I sense the exact moment when I've broken the skin. I taste metal once more as she continues to thrash in my arms, but this time I'm conscious that it's her blood in my mouth, not mine.

I can't slow down my breathing. There's so much adrenaline rushing through me that I'm not sure how much more my heart can take. Cynthia's chest rises and falls even faster than mine, so she might've reached her limit too. Her neck and face are flecked with tiny droplets of blood; I suspect mine are too.

"I hurt you," I say.

"Yes," she replies breathlessly.

"I'm sorry."

"Don't be," she says. "Let's go inside now. What floor are you on?"

"I'm in a basement studio," I admit.

She laughs, and we linger for some time in her car, our hearts still racing. "You may not believe this," she sighs, "but I almost came just then."

"Seriously? That's *fantastic!* Here, let me help you finish." I try positioning my hand underneath her skirt, but immediately she intercepts it and squeezes tightly, almost breaking my fingers.

"Even if you fucked me six ways to Sunday," she says, "that's the closest I'm ever gonna get."

*　*　*　*

I've chosen not to put this next scene into words, partly because I'm a bit of a coward and partly because I don't think my heart could stand it. If this were a movie, what I'm about to do would be the equivalent of a fade to black.

I'll try to sum it up this way: before Cynthia, sex was a puzzle to be deciphered, or, at the very least, a skill at which I lacked the necessary experience and was in desperate need of practice. But it turns out it's neither of those things. It's the *opposite* of those things.

It's telling corny jokes, listening to your favorite CDs, eating pretzels by the handful right out of the bag. It's hickeys and scratches and beer and cigarettes. It's coming inside and out, slow and fast. It's having her pull away from me all of sudden due to some longstanding, mysterious phobia she has of being smothered, then starting up again with twice the intensity once that feeling has subsided. It's kissing body parts I never thought were kissable.

And then it's over, and she showers again, but alone this time, and she dresses, and brushes her hair with my crummy, dandruff-encrusted hairbrush, and applies lipstick, and walks out the door. And she's gone.

* * * *

I've never been up to the sixteenth floor before—I've barely been out of my windowless office, holed up most days answering the phone, printing spreadsheets, and alphabetizing receipts. And so, as I make my way upstairs, I'm fairly certain that I'm headed for trouble.

A few minutes earlier, I received only my second phone call from human resources (it had been less than twenty-four hours since I received that first one, which marked my transition from temporary to permanent employee). The woman on the other end instructed me to report at once to Bob Hendrick's office for an urgent, unscheduled meeting. I didn't even get an opportunity to confer with Cynthia before heading upstairs: on most mornings, she's at her desk by eight, but, wouldn't you know it, today just happens to be the first morning since I've been at the company that she's chosen to arrive late.

The first thing I notice about the sixteenth floor is that it's a lot darker than the fifteenth, with wood paneling, stained a deep walnut, on every wall. A series of Japanese lithographs in perfect alignment with one another on either side of the hallway leads me in a straight line to the receptionist's desk.

The next thing I notice about the sixteenth floor is that it's extremely quiet up here. There isn't a cubicle in sight, and only a handful of offices, reserved for the founders, legal department, and senior management. A receptionist I don't recognize rises up from her swivel chair to guide me to Bob's office before I've even had a chance to introduce myself.

Bob Hendricks is seated behind a glass desk, waiting. Ken Lambert stands nearby, silhouetted by a massive windowpane offering a stunning view of the harbor. Japanese lithographs adorn the walls of this office as well—I'm guessing the entire floor is littered with them.

"Sit your ass down," Bob says to me.

They could be brothers, Bob and Ken, both in their fifties, both remarkably slim for men their age, dressed in nearly identical pressed blue shirts and pleated tan slacks. Bob has slightly less hair than Ken, while Ken's hair is somewhat darker than Bob's.

"You're not what I expected," Ken says to me. "Not even close."

"You've been a busy boy, haven't you Ethan?" Bob adds.

"There's plenty to do in our office, that's for sure," I answer, and they laugh in unison as if I've just told a joke.

"It's okay to let your guard down," Ken assures me. "We know everything that's been going on in that office between the two of you."

Are they talking about Cynthia? She and I had only had sex for the first time *last night*, in my *apartment*. How could they possibly know anything about *that*? Clearly they're misinformed.

"Kudos to you, my friend," Bob adds. "She's one hell of a tall glass of water."

"I fucking *love* that expression," Ken roars. "Why don't more people use it nowadays?"

"Someone ought to bring it back," Bob says. "What do you think, Ethan? Is Cynthia a tall glass of water, or what?"

"I'm not even sure what that means," I respond.

Ken laughs. "If God himself set out to invent the ultimate fuck toy," Ken says, "He'd be hard pressed to come up with a finer piece of ass than Cynthia Rhodes."

"In full agreement with you there, partner," Bob chimes in, "with one minor caveat. Not the best lay in the world, now is she?"

"Sadly, no," Ken concurs. "That crazy bitch couldn't reach orgasm if her life depended on it. But with a body like that, who gives a shit, am I right?"

"You seem like a nice kid, Ethan," Bob says. "Shame to have to lose you. We'll arrange for security to escort you out of the building."

"I'm getting fired?" I ask, finally catching on.

They turn to each other to laugh yet again, and then Bob says: "But it was worth it, right?"

"Damn straight it was worth it!" Ken replies, even though I'm assuming the question was directed at me. "And he'd do it again in a heartbeat if he had the chance. Wouldn't you, Ethan? We're not animals, you know. We've agreed to send you off with two months' severance, to give you a fighting chance."

"Okay, we're done here," Bob says.

My breath quickens as I try my best to hold back tears.

"Relax, kid," Bob adds, "we're doing you a *favor*. One day you'll thank us."

"Amen," Ken agrees. "Now get the fuck out."

* * * *

I spend the weekend waiting for Cynthia to call. Sleep hasn't been easy to come by, and I'm down to my last couple of joints.

While there's barely enough money in my bank account to pay next month's rent, the severance check I'm expecting from Hendrick and Lambert should tide me over until I can find a new source of income. I'm debating whether to ask Donna at the employment agency to place me in a new assignment, unsure at this point if I've been blacklisted by Bob and Ken. Hopefully, that's just my paranoia talking.

My health insurance is set to expire at the end of the month, but I should be eligible to extend it temporarily through COBRA. I'm seriously considering using whatever coverage I have left to visit a therapist, someone qualified to fix my life.

It's high time I started paying more attention to my personal appearance—nicer clothes, better haircuts, that sort of thing. Also, I feel like I should try to make new friends, cheerful types with bubbly personalities. Maybe I could sign up for a cooking class and connect with interesting people that way. And it might not be such a terrible idea to finally quit smoking. I could also get more exercise while I'm at it.

Life has its ups and down. I'm in a down period right now, obviously. But I can't view each setback as a permanent condition. Rather, I should look at my current situation as an *opportunity*. The universe is sending me a message. I've got to be able to find some meaning in all of this. I'll reinvent myself. I'm not obligated to remain in Boston *forever*. If all this city has to offer me are shitty temp jobs and the gradual deadening of my soul, I might as well do those things while living someplace with shorter winters, or no winters at all. I know—I'll move to *Los Angeles*, give screenwriting another shot, find redemption there. But this time it'll be different. I'll write something more marketable this time, like a romantic comedy or a psychological thriller, so I can find an agent and get my foot in the door. There's hope for me yet!

I light a fat joint and put in a Michael Penn CD before guzzling another can of beer. In my kitchen, I prepare leftover rotisserie chicken with a homemade dressing the way my father taught me to make it: Dijon mustard, extra virgin olive oil, red wine vinegar (never balsamic), fresh squeezed lemon juice, tarragon, and a crushed garlic (salt and pepper to taste). I eat standing up, painstakingly chewing each mouthful so as not to choke on any chicken bones by accident. Still hungry, I tear open a box of Petit Écolier cookies while swaying back and forth to the music. When I've finally had enough to eat, I lie on my carpeted floor, my head resting on a soft pillow, my eyelids barely open. All at once I'm able to approximate the sensation of sinking into the floor, inch by inch, noiselessly receding into the wood floorboards below the carpet and the cool concrete underneath.

Is this what dying feels like?

I start to think about God, and pretty soon I'm taunting Him with ill-advised threats. Hey *asshole*, if you're so all-powerful, why don't you just get it over with already? I won't put up a fight, that's for sure. I've had about as much of this shit as I can take.

The CD ends without warning, and the silence left in its absence makes for a fitting response.

Hey, I continue, *I'm talking to you*. This isn't funny anymore. You're really getting on my nerves. All those verses about how you giveth and taketh away—hey, were you awareth that you hadeth a slight lisp? I'd checketh into that if I were you.

I'm pretty sure the phone is ringing, but I might be imagining it. I'm marginally more confident that I'm actually reaching over to answer it, but I wouldn't bet my life on that either.

However, it appears *extremely* likely that Mr. Rhodes is speaking to me now. Either that or God has a much more gravelly voice than I would've guessed.

"Cynthia made me promise to call you," Mr. Rhodes may or may not be saying to me.

"Tell her I've moved to L.A. to become a screenwriter."

"That's a wretched idea, Ethan. You'll throw away years of your life chasing down that unfortunate pipe dream."

"What do *you* know? You're a fraud. Your entire business plan was built on sand. You made the whole thing up!"

"Guilty as charged, young man."

"You sure had me fooled, I'll give you that."

"For a time," he says to me, "I was at the center of the storm."

"Cynthia *hates* you," I sneer.

"Do you think I give a damn about that, Ethan? What kind of imbecile do you take me for?"

"Okay then, *I* hate you."

"You're a child," he barks. "For your own sake, I pray you're not suffering from the delusion that Cynthia had *feelings* for you."

"You wouldn't know the first thing about it. You never loved her, and you never understood her."

"Do you have any idea how ridiculous you sound? That woman is incapable of loving *anyone*."

"I had *sex* with her, Mr. Rhodes! I had sex with your wife! What do you think of that?"

"I hold no grudges. You were a deer caught in the headlights from the very start."

"Can't you at least have the decency to be jealous?"

"Because you slept with my wife? She's been passed around like a hot potato by half the men I know—why should you be any different?"

"You're despicable, Mr. Rhodes, you know that? You really are the worst."

"She left me, Ethan. She moved out this morning. She quit her job too. I have no idea where she went."

"Maybe she's planning on moving in with *me*—ever think of that?"

"Ethan, stop being such a goddamned fool. She's the one who insisted I contact you. She gave me your telephone number, for crying out loud. It was the only favor she asked of me, and I've agreed to comply."

"I'm confused," I tell him.

"She wrote you a note, which I'm to read to you now over the telephone. Are you paying attention? Because I'm only doing this once. 'Dear Ethan, I can wipe it all away'..." He stops reading. "Wipe it all away," he scoffs. "What a hackneyed turn of phrase."

"Just *read* it, Mr. Rhodes."

"Apologies. 'Dear Ethan, I can wipe it all away. I can leave this city, change my name, meet a man someday with a heart as big as yours, maybe even start a family'...a *family*? Have you ever heard such drivel?"

"Shut *up*, Mr. Rhodes!"

"'...Maybe even start a family. The simple silly things that grownups do. I assumed it was too late for me, that I'd missed my chance. But then you went and fell out of the sky. I can't begin to explain the impact you've had on me. All I can say is that you've made it possible somehow for me to put aside the things I needed to forget. I'm so terribly sorry, Ethan. You deserved better than this. Please understand that I could never have said these words to you in person. But I'll make you a promise. Someone is out there, waiting for you, Ethan, and whatever strange effect you've had on me she'll one day have on you. And then it will be your turn to wipe it all away, and do the simple silly things that grownups do.'"

1994

PROBLEMS IN THAT DEPARTMENT

Russell arranges to meet her twice a week, for coffee, never lunch, in the office cafeteria, where they speak without fervor of bygone hairstyles, fantasy ice cream flavors, and the high cost of a decent pair of sneakers. He impresses her with jokes pilfered from a CD-ROM, trying his best to attain separation from his lingering emotional baggage. Jenna Cleary is passing several uneventful summer months with the company as a temporary clerical assistant in the accounting department. It's a miserable chore, she assures him, although Russell can't imagine a fate substantially worse than his: two years spent sorting interoffice memoranda in the mailroom of their nondescript Boston brokerage firm.

According to Jenna, the pasty, bearded women of accounts payable have a knack for sucking the youth and vibrancy out of new employees. Previous assistants are rumored to have gained ten pounds within a single accounting quarter, ballooning to extraordinary proportions by the close of fiscal year. In the break room one August afternoon, Jenna slams her palm onto a formica countertop and confides in Russell, "I'm aging in *dog years*."

The waning days of Jenna's stint at the company are fast approaching. Come autumn, she'll drive out to the University of California at Berkeley to begin a six year Ph.D. program in history, economics, or possibly both— Russell made inquiries early on in their friendship and promptly forgot her response.

Layer cake, soda, and clusters of fat women descend upon the cafeteria to mark Jenna's last day at the firm. She catches sight of Russell at a window and inexplicably—at least as far as he's concerned—rushes over to greet him, depositing in his shirt pocket a torn piece of paper on which she's scribbled her address.

"I know it's short notice," she whispers to him, "but a few friends are dropping by tonight to see me off."

Clutching a six-pack of beer, Russell makes the long trek from the nearest subway station to a vinyl-sided three-family relic near Teal Square, in Somerville, where he spots Jenna waving to him from her front porch as he fumbles with the latch on the chain-link fence surrounding her residence. Dressed in tight blue jeans and a cashmere sweater, she's the prettiest girl who has waved exclusively to Russell in a very long time. *Don't let me be the first to arrive*, Russell pleads to no one in particular, an instant before it dawns on him that Jenna wouldn't be waiting alone on her front porch if she had other guests to attend to.

They sit crosslegged on her uncarpeted living room floor encircled by flickering candles, a wall of empty beer cans amassing between them. Other than the candles, everything Jenna owns is either en route by United Parcel Service to Berkeley or crammed into her Nissan Sentra parked across the street—and pretty soon the candles will be melted and gone.

After the six-pack has been consumed but not entirely absorbed into their bloodstreams, her friends still unaccounted for, she says, "would you take it the wrong way if I kissed you?" Russell shivers from a partly real and partly imagined gust of cold air. They kiss, and ten minutes later he's tying a knot at the end of his condom to keep his sperm from dribbling out. A cheerless and icy mood permeates the room. Jenna tucks the tank-top that was previously hidden underneath her sweater back into her jeans.

"You'd better get going; you need to be at work tomorrow," she remarks after another round of well-mannered kissing. It's the first time Russell can recall a girl ever feeding *him* the excuse he needed to make his escape. He responds in kind: "Yeah, I guess you've got a long trip ahead of you."

Later that night, back in his apartment and unable to fall asleep, he determines that the ten minutes of bad sex he had with Jenna was rooted in the timing, that they each held back emotionally to avoid any potential entanglements on the eve of her departure.

Fast forward to January, and Russell, drunk on the byproduct of too much gin and trace quantities of tonic water, has an image stuck in his head of his jeans down by his ankles and Jenna asking if he'd just ejaculated because he'd been so quiet that she wasn't sure. For a while now, Russell has been experiencing flashbacks from that late summer night on Jenna's creaking wooden floor. Lately, however, it's gotten a bit out of hand; he can't seem to shake Jenna, or California, from his thoughts. Maybe she had the right idea, relocating as she did, away from the snow banks, dirty slush, and freezing temperatures of another interminable Boston winter. Holed up under a fleece blanket with his telephone, he dials the operator and asks for the number of "Genna Cleery" in Berkeley, spelling both her first and last name incorrectly.

"I have a Jenna with a J and a Cleary with an A," the operator offers, almost as a consolation.

"Sure, might as well take it," Russell mutters, crestfallen, convinced it must be the wrong person.

Jenna answers after the second ring and he jumps right into it: take a break from winter, never been to Frisco, or is it San Fran, crash on her sofa?

"I live in a studio apartment," she tells him, once he's paused long enough for her to get the words out. "I don't have a ton of space."

"I don't mind," Russell says.

"You'd be a half-hour BART ride from the city."

"I don't mind," he repeats, by now feeling quite nauseous.

"I'll have my hands full trying to make up an incomplete. We wouldn't be able to spend much time together."

"Honestly, Jenna," he cries out, "*I don't mind.*"

Hanging up the phone, he's not entirely sure whether she extended a clear-cut invitation to him or not. Unable to reach a definitive conclusion, he nonetheless calls an airline to book his flight. A few days later—two weeks, in fact, before his twenty-seventh birthday—he arrives at the San Francisco International Airport, not quite certain if Jenna will be there to greet him.

He spots her straightaway, reading a newspaper on the benches near baggage claim. They take tentative steps toward the other, culminating in an unremarkable hug, and she teases him, or at least he hopes she's teasing, that she was afraid of not being able to recognize him. He presents her with the requisite T-shirt and mug picked up at Logan, then trails a few steps behind her to a distant parking lot where her Sentra is located. Slumped low in her passenger seat, Russell stares wordlessly out the window as they cross the Bay Bridge, heading away from San Francisco.

The sky brightens as if on cue the moment they reach Berkeley, and she suggests they take an impromptu walking tour of her neighborhood and the campus before heading over to her apartment. Russell, tying his sweatshirt around his waist, can't get over how much warmer it is in Berkeley than San Francisco. They weave in and out of record stores and used clothing boutiques on Shattuck and Telegraph Streets, making quick stops in between to pick up locally grown organic tomatoes at a produce collective, fresh mozzarella at a cheese collective, and a round loaf of sourdough at a bread collective. Then it's onto the original Peet's coffee shop, where Russell orders an iced latté, and Blondie's, where they share a slice of mushroom pizza.

The sidewalks are teeming with locals, and Russell, feeling upbeat, tosses a quarter to a drugged-out bum wearing a yellow and teal tie-dye shirt. There's much to see in all directions: Russell can't help but gawk at hand-holding lesbians, bug-eyed student activists passing out flyers, white boys in dreadlocks, and forty-year-old professorial-types smoking joints outside non-denominational churches. The groups seem linked somehow, a collection of animatronic characters on a psychedelic theme park ride. "It's like we're in Hippieland at Disney World!" Russell blurts out, realizing a split second too late that he probably should have kept that comment to himself.

Sidestepping a yin-yang symbol drawn in chalk on the sidewalk, Russell tries to summon what he's picked up over the years about Zen Buddhism and Taoism (pronounced with a *D*, not a *T*, he once learned the hard way). Most of what springs to mind are nonsensical bits and pieces about inner peace, finding bliss, that sort of thing. There might've been something about setting realistic expectations for himself—or perhaps not setting any expectations at all—but Russell never bothered to commit that sort of thing to memory.

By the time they circle back to the car, it's gotten so hot outside that both of them are sweating. Driving home, Jenna volunteers to slow down as they pass Chez Panisse, but Russell, having never heard of the place, reacts with indifference. In a makeshift garden behind her building, Jenna picks sprigs of basil and mint, and, once inside her apartment, serves him chilled mango iced tea with a single mint leaf floating on top. His brain might be playing tricks on him, but he's pretty sure he can taste mint in every sip. Later, she serves the soft mozzarella and tomato slices on a bed of butter lettuce, topped with basil from her garden and a drizzle of extra virgin olive oil. Russell can't remember anything ever tasting so delicious, and helps himself to another slice of sourdough to use like a sponge to wipe his plate clean. It's all too much for him—the January heat, Jenna, the garden herbs and just-baked bread. As soon as she gets up from the table, he jumps to his feet to join her, maneuvering to land a kiss somewhere in the vicinity of her lips. Jenna skillfully manages to glide past him at the last possible instant, causing him to barrel into the refrigerator instead.

"Do we have to do this now?" she teases, turning away to bring their dirty dishes to the sink.

"No, of course not," he says. "I just thought we'd pick up where we left off."

"Let's not get ahead of ourselves," she laughs.

Russell experiences a wave of jet lag-induced exhaustion as the late afternoon sun descends behind clusters of eucalyptus trees. Jenna advises him to take a short nap on her lumpy futon, explaining that everyone in Berkeley stays out late anyway so he won't be missing anything. He manages a few hours of restless sleep, after which they catch the ten o'clock showing of the new Bruce Willis movie. They're surrounded in the auditorium by an audience of Kerouac hipsters in suede jackets and colored beads, who, when the movie lets out, congregate outside the theater to share their opinions. Russell and Jenna, both famished, devour a combination platter of sushi and tempura at her favorite Japanese spot—still bustling past midnight—before climbing a steep hill through faint mist to the public rose gardens overlooking the city.

Back in her apartment just before three o'clock in the morning, Jenna changes into a pair of plaid pajamas and immerses herself in a thin paperback entitled "Only Words." Russell, laying beside her now on her futon, contemplates reaching over to caress her stomach, her elbow—her stomach, her elbow?—thinks better of it, and instead spends the next hour scanning the minutiae of her stucco ceiling long after she's switched off the lights.

He experiences each new day with Jenna as more strained and bewildering than the last. At one point, she proposes a trip to Napa Valley for a wine tasting, but they hardly say a word to each other the whole ride up. He can't seem to snap out of his sullen mood, though he comes close while posing for pictures in front of Francis Ford Coppola's *Godfather* Oscars, temporarily on display in the gift shop of the filmmaker's winery.

On the drive home, she makes a detour to the Headlands, north of the Golden Gate Bridge, from where they're able to hike down a path leading to Drakes Bay. As they make their way to the shore, Jenna points out sea otters lounging on jutting rocks. It's nearing sunset, and their view of the bridge and city from across the shimmering water is nothing short of spectacular; but Russell kicks at sand and pretends to be unimpressed, asking her why they didn't visit the "really big trees" instead.

Later, they eat take-out salads in silence on the edge of her futon while watching TV. It's a detective show, with a murder to solve, and, as soon as the culprit is revealed, Jenna shuts off the TV and pulls a blanket over her head. Russell tries to give her as much space as the cramped bed will allow, but ends up so close to the edge of the futon that he's afraid he'll roll off in the middle of the night.

Jet-lag and a general sense of dread gets the best of him that night, and he falls into a deep sleep for the next ten hours. When he finally opens his eyes, Jenna's nowhere to be seen, and his mood only worsens (if that's even possible). Spotting a San Francisco guidebook and a spare key to her apartment on the kitchen counter, he sighs, resigned to the notion that he ought to visit San Francisco proper at least once during his stay.

He rides the BART into the city and plods up and down sloping streets and alleyways in no specific direction for much of the afternoon. He loses his breath often, either from the sheer grade of certain hilltop climbs, or, to a lesser degree—and perhaps somewhat self-consciously—from the stunning panoramic charm of his surroundings. In the Haight, he buys a hippie chain and decides to keep moving west, through Golden Gate Park, until reaching the ocean, where the faint outlines of a plan begins to take shape in his mind as he sits cross-legged on the sand while touching seawater with his fingertips: substitute his Boston Financial

District mailroom position for a San Francisco Financial District mailroom position, find a cheap basement apartment at the bottom of some hill in the Haight, the Mission, or Cole Valley, grow his hair long, smoke more weed than usual, learn to play the acoustic guitar, read primers on Eastern philosophy, take an axe to his fears and insecurities, split them like firewood, burn them to ashes and hurl them into the wind.

And then he thinks of Jenna. *She's all wrong for me anyway*, he decides. She's wholesome, cheerful, well adjusted. It hardly escapes his notice that she's objectively smarter than he is as well, with six years of intensive research and instruction awaiting her, to be followed, as she once put it, by another six to ten years of unremitting grief on the bumpy road to tenure (Russell's still in the dark about her particular field of study). The other night, she referenced the Galápagos Islands, and Russell chimed in, "Galápagos? You mean where they discovered Social Darwinism?"

Upon his return to Berkeley, he finds her napping on her futon and tries his best not to wake her.

"Did you have fun?" she mumbles from across the room, her eyes still closed.

"It's a beautiful city," he answers.

"I don't get there as often as I'd like."

"I have a lot on my mind, Jenna."

"No kidding."

"Could we talk about it?" His voice cracks.

"Oh brother, here we go," she says. "I had a feeling this was coming."

"You already know what I'm gonna say?"

"I'm afraid so," she replies. "You don't exactly have a poker face. Hey, has anyone ever mentioned to you that you have a one-track mind?"

Many people, in fact, have made this observation to Russell before.

"Let me save you some time," she continues. "We're not all meant to be compatible with everyone else. You and I, we're just not a good match. We gave it our best shot that night in Boston, but the moment passed, and now you just need to accept that it's not especially important to me whether we have sex or not."

"It's important to me."

"No kidding," she says. "You lie in my bed with that frown of yours, that painful squint in your eye. It's like you're sitting on death row, praying to have your sentence commuted."

"Was it really so bad that first time?"

"No one wants an honest answer to a question like that," she tells him.

"Can't we have one more go at it?"

"Is that why you flew all the way out here, Russell, to have sex with me again?"

"No! I was long overdue for a vacation, and I've always wanted to visit Northern California. Also, I thought it would be fun to spend a few days with you."

"This hasn't exactly been my idea of fun."

"You don't like me very much, do you?"

"We hardly know each other," she reminds him.

"You think I'm stupid."

"Where'd you get that idea?"

"I'm not stupid."

"I never said you were stupid."

"You don't take me seriously," he says.

"That's not it at all. Isn't it obvious by now that we're not meant to be together? I'm sorry you had to fly three thousand miles to find that out, but it's the truth."

"So that's the reason—that we're incompatible? It's not that you think I'm lousy in bed?"

"Moving on to the next topic!" she insists.

"Because I can be good in bed, Jenna. I just want to make that clear."

"Noted, thank you."

"And anyway," he adds, "I'm a quick learner."

"*Study*," she corrects him. "Quick study."

"What I'm trying to say is that I know there's room for improvement."

"Glad you think so," she says.

"Jesus, Jenna, it's not like I'm one of those replicants from *Blade Runner* who doesn't know he's a replicant. Give me another chance!"

She shrugs. "That reference means nothing to me. I rented the director's cut years ago and it put me straight to sleep."

"Seriously?" he snaps. "Jesus, how could you fall asleep?"

She exhales with a whistle.

"Fine," he says. "You're right. You're right about all of it. Dammit, how did I even end up here?"

"You drunk-called me last week, don't you remember? Did you think I was gonna be your long distance girlfriend or something?"

"It crossed my mind," he says. "I'm sorry, Jenna. I must be a lot lonelier than I thought. I'm pretty sure I need help." He stands up suddenly. "Will somebody please fucking *help* me?" He sits down again.

"Unfortunately for you, I'm in the wrong Ph.D. program for any of that," she says. "By the way, you're sleeping on the couch tonight."

They work out an arrangement—that is, Jenna establishes the ground rules and Russell agrees to comply. He's scheduled to depart in a few days; until then, he's prohibited from attempting to engage Jenna in any sort of heartfelt dialogue of the pained confessional variety. Moreover, he's not permitted to brood. He can expect to fend for himself during the remainder of his stay, as she plans to pass the bulk of that time at the university library completing work on a term paper, and he's to presume, unless notified to the contrary, that she'll be making her own dinner plans. Her car is off-limits, naturally, and he's not to answer her telephone under any circumstances. Also, he will not be getting a ride to the airport.

Jenna spends her waking hours away from the apartment and away from him. Russell eats dinner the following night at a cheap Mexican dive on Shattuck, killing time afterwards at a used bookstore where he pretends somewhat halfheartedly to be a graduate student. He doesn't return to her apartment until he's confident she's already asleep, and, stumbling in the darkness, locates the blanket and pillow she's put out for him on the sofa.

The morning of his departure, she drives him to the airport after all, as a reward for what she deems his good behavior. She double-parks near a string of taxicabs, extends a perfunctory handshake, and speeds off. At the ticket counter, an airline representative glances at Russell's ticket and can't stop laughing. A blizzard in the Northeast dumped two feet of snow in the Boston area —"didn't you catch the news?"

Russell waits an hour before calling Jenna.

"You're not gonna believe this," he says, "but I can't go home."

"You can't stay *here*."

"Thought so. Have a nice life, all that crap."

"Manipulative bastard."

"I'm not trying to manipulate you," he says, "at least I don't think I am. I'm stuck in San Francisco for the next twenty-four hours and I'm completely out of cash. I'm sorry I was such a lousy lay in Boston, and I'm sorry for obsessing about having sex with you again during this trip. I'm sorry about the weather back east too, in case I had anything to do with *that*."

"Do me a favor," she says. "Apologize in advance to the next girl you meet."

"You think it'll help?"

Within the hour, Russell finds himself once more slumped low in the passenger seat of her Sentra, crossing the Bay Bridge to Berkeley. But things feel different this time. As far as Jenna's concerned, he's on a flight back to Boston, and she refers to the person seated next to her as "The Ghost of His Former Self." She warns him that ghosts don't speak, "so don't make a sound if you know what's good for you." She stops at a drugstore for bathroom supplies, takes him along, picks up a houseplant at a nursery, takes him along. She takes him everywhere she needs to go. Undressing in the middle of the afternoon, she presses the weight of her warm body firmly against his, and he's inside of her before they've even reached the bed. Again and again, she calls him her own private ghost, a figment of her imagination, says he isn't really there, it isn't really him.

1995

WHAT BASEBALL IS FOR

At half past seven, end-of-day sunlight intruding on the club on the rare occasion its front doors swing open and shut, Asia Minor has so few customers it can scarcely be considered open for business. Stu Riskin, hunched over the bar, is nursing his second gin and tonic when the women, five in total, pass through the swinging doors. Initially, he's too worn out, killing time at the end of another dreary week, to reposition his intractable frame toward the club's creaky stage where the five women have assembled. But their sudden emergence in an otherwise dormant bar registers acutely enough in his peripheral vision to warrant the exertion.

Biologically speaking, Stu remains well shy of thirty; emotionally, the span is much wider. At the present time, Stu has yet to discover that the women, members of a local all-girl lingerie rock band known as The Vulvas, are scheduled, within a few short hours, to swap their street clothes for red and black satin lingerie, taut garter belts, steel-toed army boots, and knee-high athletic socks. The keyboardist will discard her baseball cap to reveal a fresh buzzcut, the lead singer with spiked hair will apply multicolored sparkles to her already noteworthy chest, the drummer will roll a pack of Lucky Strikes into the sleeve of her meticulously torn T-shirt, and the lead guitarist will hook a complex array of metal rings through her nose, eyebrows, and lower lip. Only the bass player, Miranda Trilby, all but spilling out of her sage green floral-print sundress with spaghetti straps and descending button work, will take the stage without any significant modification.

Earlier that evening, at the Watertown diner where the women gathered to bulk up on pasta and eggs before their gig, Miranda stunned her bandmates with the news that she'd be quitting The Vulvas at the end of the summer to attend business school at Babson College. They all assumed she was joking. Business school? What the hell is *that?* The band stood poised on the verge of nominal success in Boston's alternative rock scene, beneficiaries of the continued rise in popularity of grunge music in 1994 and a more generalized acceptance within mainstream culture of so-called "lipstick lesbians" as sexually desirable to straight men.

It wasn't all that unusual for Miranda to express her displeasure with the band. For a while now, she'd been fed up by their provocative costumes and erotically-charged lyrics (no less than three of their songs celebrated the masturbatory pleasures of battery operated sex toys)—but tonight was the first time she voiced her intention to hang up the lingerie for good. Her bandmates took great offense at any suggestion their act might somehow be degrading towards women, pointing out to Miranda that lingerie grunge bands aren't subject to accusations of sexual exploitation for the simple reason that any woman who expands the boundaries of her own sexuality willingly and voluntarily cannot by definition be considered a participant in her own debasement.

But Miranda's mind was made up—business school, end of story. She was willing to be flexible about her end-date, offering to honor any previously scheduled concerts until her replacement could be found. But she refused to budge regarding the outfit she'd wear onstage from this point forward: no more lingerie for Miranda. Her new look, to be debuted at tonight's gig, featured a sage green floral-print sundress with spaghetti straps and descending button work (the dress was made from a wrinkle-free synthetic fabric that could be washed and squeeze-dried between shows). "Guys have told me they think it's hot," she stressed, "chicks too."

The rest of her bandmates viewed Miranda's revolt against satin and lace undergarments as an undeserved renunciation of their deeply held convictions—"it's like admitting our lingerie was never intended to express any sort of political ideology whatsoever," the lead singer argued—and a compromise of sorts was reached, granting Miranda use of the sundress on stage provided it remained halfway unbuttoned at all times.

From Stu's perspective at the bar, as one of a handful of young, hip, smart, funny, good-natured, open-minded men in a mostly empty club, the arrival of not one but *five* women presents an ideal platform from which to convey his aforementioned virtues in a surprisingly uncompetitive environment. He scans the stage from his barstool perch before fixing his gaze on the girl in the beige dress (he's red-green color-blind, and sage is a particularly challenging color for him).

Stu's heart sinks momentarily as Beige Dress and another girl break away and *exit the bar*, leaving him to ponder whether their departure somehow reflects poorly on him. Undeterred, he gulps down whatever's left of his warm, diluted gin and tonic and shifts his attention to the three remaining women, specifically the one with spiked hair and vast hips, her breasts shapelier and more substantial than he initially gave her credit for.

Beige Dress returns, seconds later, guitar case and duffle bag in tow, and Stu springs into action, is in fact the only man in the entire club to do so—a turn of events he attributes to his superior powers of perception.

"Need a hand?" he asks Beige Dress, bounding forward.

"Are you Larry?"

"No, I'm Stu."

"They told us Larry would help us unload."

"Fuck Larry. I'm your man."

Over the next half-hour, Stu lugs amplifiers, instrument cases, and microphone stands from the group's van, double-parked on Massachusetts Avenue, to the stage, and back again, five or six more times, until there's so much dirt and grime smeared onto his polyester shirt that he resembles a beleaguered hero in an action movie.

By the time the concert gets underway, a little after ten o'clock, the arrival of a hundred paying customers erases any remnants of tedium from the club. The audience seems both drunk and enthusiastic during the band's set, though mostly drunk. Sadly, no amount of alcohol can mask how shockingly bad The Vulvas sound. They're *awful*, fusing musical styles that, in more capable hands, would have been deliberately kept apart. Stu recognizes a Latin influence, Deep Purple, some Sinatra, and, of course, a healthy dose of grunge, the sum total of which achieves a dissonant muddiness pleasing to no one. Stu can't dance to it—though, to be fair, he can't dance to much of anything—and, in any event, gives up after the first tune, once he realizes he's close enough to the stage to have his movements scrutinized by Miranda.

Her green/beige dress, unbuttoned now practically to her navel, reveals quick, tantalizing flashes of skin almost as an afterthought.

No one other than Stu seems to be paying much attention to Miranda: by and large, the men and women in the audience appear mesmerized by the lead singer instead. Her tremendous, heaving breasts sparkle like disco balls each time she moves in and out of a dedicated spotlight. Dressed only in racy lingerie and army boots, she bounces up and down on stage with such erotic intensity that it catches Stu off guard. All along, Miranda, bored and glassy-eyed, stares ahead at nothing in particular, her face frozen in an expression Stu interprets as openly hostile, her body swaying to rhythms disassociated from whatever it is the rest of her band is hoping to accomplish.

The Vulvas's set functions as a kind of reverse aphrodisiac for Stu: his attraction to Miranda was a lot stronger before the concert got underway. When the house lights are switched back on—band members dispersing promptly in five separate directions—Stu either volunteers or is enlisted to carry equipment back out to the van. Afterwards, his shirt untucked, he reconnects with Miranda outside the club as she lights a cigarette.

"Think there's pudding in the fridge?" she asks, pointing inside.

"I suppose it's possible, though I didn't see it on the menu."

"Come on," she laughs, grabbing Stu by the arm and pulling him toward the darkened kitchen behind the bar.

They kiss right away, Miranda first leaning against then resting atop a cool aluminum countertop. Hardly able to believe his good fortune, Stu runs through in his mind all the assorted techniques he's picked up over the years for handling the nipple. He bites playfully, sucks, licks, etc., and, once he's done with all that, presses her breasts together as if he's trying to combine them into one. Miranda tilts her head back, which Stu takes as a good sign, and next thing he knows she's inquiring as to the existence of a condom in his wallet. Things are moving pretty fast, and soon she's unzipping his fly and pulling out his penis, gripping onto it firmly and rubbing it back and forth against her hips. Before he can figure out how to slow down his brain, he's already ejaculated onto her sundress.

Miranda shoves him away to clean herself off, washing the affected areas of her dress at a nearby sink. Stu notices a few beads of his sperm still clinging to a hard-to-reach spot on the back of her dress and offers to wipe them off with a handy dish towel.

"I should've known you'd be a squirter," she remarks.

"I'm truly fucking sorry."

"You could have *warned* me."

"I know. I feel lousy."

"Well, you're gonna feel even worse when I tell you this next part. Before we were about to fuck on that metal countertop over there, I was gonna suck your dick."

"Oh my God," he replies, dumbfounded. "Is there anything I can do to make it up to you?"

"You mean sexually, or are you offering to take me shopping for a new dress?"

"Both?"

She fusses with her hair. "Shit, I have to get back to the van, otherwise my bandmates will ditch me first chance they get."

"Miranda, wait. Don't you think...I mean, shouldn't we..."

"I have to go."

"I'm not so bad to have around," he blurts out.

"You sure about that?"

"I could be your personal roadie. Or groupie. I'll edit your goddamned newsletter, if that's what it takes."

"It's a bit too late for that, I'm afraid. I'm quitting the band next month."

His head swims in a potent mixture of alcohol, lust, and regret as he fights to string words together. "Tell me what to say, Miranda," is the best he can come up with as she prepares to exit the kitchen.

She stops fidgeting and turns to him. "Well, I could sure use a friend at a party tonight," she answers.

"Everyone's headed there now, but none of the other girls will speak to me."

"Perfect," he shoots back, "I love parties. Need a lift?"

It's a ten minute drive in his gray-bronze Saturn SL1 to an East Cambridge loft, owned, Stu learns along the way, by a recent MIT graduate whose start-up company wrote sections of multi-platform code for something called the hypertext transfer protocol. The guy apparently belonged to a group of MIT students a few years back who sold their code to Microsoft for a hefty sum, and ended up purchasing the top unit of a converted warehouse that overlooks the Charles River. Stu, who for the past six months has been setting up slide projectors in hotel conference rooms for eleven bucks an hour, thinks Miranda must be mistaken: who in their right mind would be crazy enough to live in a warehouse in *East Cambridge*? She smokes a cigarette while crossing and uncrossing her legs. "Anyway," she says, perhaps sensing his skepticism, "he's rich as hell and extremely generous with his drugs."

Stu was wrong about the neighborhood. Each aging industrial lot they pass is bookended by a series of increasingly expansive construction sites; every structure along the way is either in the process of getting torn down or built up.

The warehouse in question has maintained its original brick exterior, but everything else has been replaced by steel and glass. There's an elevator encased in thick slabs of glass in the lobby, but Miranda refuses to wait for it; as they climb the stairwell to the top floor, she's accosted by one grinning man after another, the majority of whom are taller than Stu, with better hair. Each man they pass seems acquainted with Miranda, perhaps intimately; one after the next wraps his arms around her slender waist and plants a kiss on her eagerly proffered cheek.

Stu assumes he'll track Miranda at the party, hovering close-at-hand; instead, he loses sight of her straightaway. He catches glimpses of her as she darts, like a pinball in a dress, from one corner of the massive open space to another, embracing various men and women in her path. Stu guzzles down a Heineken from the kitchen and opens a second one before migrating through a cornfield of fluid bodies to a towering window overlooking the Charles.

His ears continue to buzz from standing too near to the amplifiers at the concert, and now the pulsating beats emitting from invisible loudspeakers threaten to explode his brain. With Miranda gone, he's alert to the presence of other members of her band, is careful to avoid them. Eventually, he cozies up to a faction of agreeable pot smokers and resigns himself to the prospect of a consolation high.

Darren is a talent agent's assistant visiting from Los Angeles. Karl is a square-jawed bartender attending culinary school in the fall. Samantha conducts research in molecular biology at Tufts University. Philip, it turns out, is another of those MIT grads Miranda talked about who got rich off computer code. Recognizing he can't compete in terms of pedigree with any of his newfound acquaintances, Stu avoids telling them what he does for a living, and pretty soon they forget to ask. After a time, someone passes him the most colossal joint he's ever seen.

By his third hit, he's leaning against the ceiling-high window to keep from falling on his face. Meanwhile, Philip, the brilliant MIT nerd, excites a swelling crowd with tales of a burgeoning technology already commonplace at every computer science lab in the country that has the potential to change the course of human evolution. "Our focus remains squarely on the here and now," he stresses, "enabling academics, scientists, and philosophers to share in the free and open exchange of ideas. But we're up against the clock. We don't have the luxury anymore to wait for future generations to ride in like the calvary to save us from ourselves. Civilization doesn't have that kind of time to spare."

It does no good for Stu to keep paying attention. If it was already a struggle making sense of webs, nets, and highways before the exceptionally powerful weed kicked in, by now the task is Herculean. Lurching in the direction of a nearby credenza, he perceives his torso descending gracefully onto the cold tile flooring, where he's met, after a brief repose, by Karl, the square-jawed bartender, who seems curious to learn how Stu ended up at the party.

"Miranda," Stu groans.

"Miranda Trilby? Holy Christ," Karl laughs. "You poor fucking bastard. Tell me everything."

"Rain check," Stu says with considerable effort.

Miranda finds him there, on the floor—he's not sleeping, but he's not entirely awake either—and she manages to pour a few drops of ice water down his throat.

"I see you've been making friends," she says, crouching beside him.

"I smoked something."

"You did indeed," she replies.

"I should probably get some sleep."

"Yes, but in a bed." She gestures to Karl, who's been watching intently from nearby, for assistance in getting Stu to his feet, and the three of them ride the elevator downstairs to the lobby. "Let's get that drink soon," Karl says to Miranda, who offers no response.

Miranda fishes through Stu's pockets for his car keys, then, pressing her palm against the small of his back, guides him toward his Saturn and deposits him in the passenger seat before speeding off in an unknowable direction. Stu doesn't revive again until Miranda has shut off the engine—a breach in time he can't hope to account for. Their halting strides toward her building and up three flights of spiraling staircase are similarly indistinct. Inside her apartment at last, she leads him down a pitch black hallway without bothering to switch on a light.

Left alone to fend for himself in what is presumably her bedroom, he stumbles over to her bed, leaving him barely enough stamina in reserve to pull off his shoes and socks. Hypnotic splashing sounds issue from an adjacent bathroom. By the time he gets around to unbuckling his belt, he's almost drifted off to sleep.

Miranda reappears just then, removing his pants and underwear in one fluid motion. She falters somewhat as she tries to pull off his shirt without unbuttoning it first; the collar catches temporarily around his neck, startling him out of his reverie long enough to observe that she isn't wearing any clothes.

Stu is fairly certain he won't get another chance like this one. Not in this lifetime. But nestled in her arms and legs and pressed firmly against her beating chest, underneath sheets twice as thick as anything he's used to, it feels exhilarating somehow to thumb his nose at God. Fingers stray, hair is caught, knees fold sensibly into warm spaces, but only sleep awaits.

He opens his eyes to an empty and unfamiliar place, sunlight crashing through a window. The first thing that catches his attention, other than the absence of Miranda, is how clean and organized her apartment is—a far cry from his chaotic basement studio. Her toothbrush sits inside a porcelain mug on an otherwise bare shelf above the bathroom sink. In the kitchen, dishes are lined up according to height in the drying rack. There seems to be a kind of underlying logic behind the placement of all her things, thereby making the lack of any note left for him all the more conspicuous.

Stu peels a grapefruit, and, still hungry, helps himself to a slice of toast with jam. Without any logical rationale for remaining in her apartment, he runs his fingers through his unruly hair and dresses in yesterday's clothes before sitting down at her kitchen table to compose a note of his own:

Dear Miranda,

Thanks for rescuing me last night and letting me sleep it off. I'm not sure what felt more surreal, listening to a lingerie grunge band, partying with MIT millionaires, or spending time with you. There wasn't a single moment during the entire evening when I had any idea what I was doing—so I guess it's only fitting that I woke up with no clue where I am. I'll leave you my number, in case you feel like getting in touch.

Fondly,

Stu Riskin

Descending Miranda's winding staircase to the lobby below, he exits her building and immediately spies his Saturn at the far end of the street. But where is he? What city is this? Determined not to get behind the wheel until he knows more about his surroundings, he walks in the direction of the nearest traffic light in search of familiar landmarks. Eventually, he comes to recognize a bar and pizza joint that he frequented in college, signaling his close proximity to Cleveland Circle.

He's about to double-back to his Saturn when he spots a baseball diamond on the opposite side of the intersection. Two uniformed amateur teams are in the middle of a game, and Stu, having nothing better to do, crosses the street to watch an inning or two.

The players are predominantly Hispanic, shouting in Spanish from their benches or from the on-deck circles. Both teams are comprised of college-aged men, although a few of them might be as old as Stu. The bats are aluminum, clanking each time someone makes contact with a pitch. More than an inning passes before either team succeeds in getting a runner on base.

Nothing about the game resembles a televised contest. Runners swerve when they're supposed to be sprinting in a straight line. Errors are committed with startling regularity, and batters keep getting plunked on the shoulder or forearm from pitches way out of the strike zone. Baseballs are mostly fouled off, or, if put into play, bounce five or six times in the dirt before reaching an infielder. Catchers on both teams drop an inordinate number of fastballs, including strikes, right down the middle of the plate. On the rare occasion that a pitcher attempts to throw a curveball, the baseball seems to lack the required velocity to reach home plate before slipping underneath the catcher's mitt and rolling meekly to the backstop.

Stu keeps his distance, leaning against a parking meter about twenty yards from the diamond. A handful of spectators—girlfriends of the players, mostly, chatting amongst themselves in Spanish—look on, but they're much closer to the action, cheering from metal benches behind a chain-link fence on the edge of the grass. Stu finds himself applauding whenever a line drive is caught or a base is stolen. A scuffle breaks out after yet another batter is hit by an errant pitch, and Stu trots over to the field for a closer look.

1995

ACKNOWLEDGEMENTS

It feels awkward these decades removed to acknowledge those who once impacted my work, but here we are. I'd like to begin by thanking the literary agent who did everything she could to find a publisher for my first novel in 1993. I wouldn't trade those precious moments when it seemed as if my life was about to change for anything in the world.

The generosity and encouragement I received from Jay Neugeboren, my writing professor at UMass, felt crucial, both during and after college. What a blessing it was for a young writer to be mentored by a novelist as gifted and inspiring as Jay!

Many friends and fellow writers played significant roles during that time as well, but none more so than Tim Bartell, who offered me invaluable insights and, to this day, remains one of my closest friends. And special thanks go to Dana Garvey for volunteering to read this manuscript with a critical eye prior to its publication, identifying mistakes that had been hiding in plain sight from the very start.

I can't sufficiently express my gratitude to my wife, Nicole, for all her love and support. She had heard about the old stories I kept in boxes in our basement, but presumed she'd never get a chance to read them. I had no way of knowing how she'd react to these unvarnished glimpses into my past; happily, it turns out I had nothing to fear.

ABOUT THE AUTHOR

Jerome Stern wrote his first short story as a teenager and his last one when he was nearing thirty, in 1995. That's when he quit writing fiction once and for all to lead a "normal" life instead. Over a ten-year stretch, Jerome wrote a slacker novel set in Los Angeles, numerous screenplays featuring indecisive main characters, and dozens of stories, including the title novella of this collection, "Little Did He Know."

A husband and father, Jerome lives in the Boston area, where he works as a video producer and editor. At some point he may take up writing fiction again, but he's careful not to get his hopes up.

contact@breaktheroad.com

www.ingramcontent.com/pod-product-compliance
Lightning Source LLC
Chambersburg PA
CBHW021115110726
47900CB00007B/2197